HE SAID, "YOU DESTROYED THE BODY, DIDN'T YOU?"

He was a small man, quite frail, with yellow wrinkled skin. Little simian eyes peered at me through thick lenses. I figured him for seventy, maybe eighty. His name was Mr. Primavera and I knew I'd seen it in the newspapers.

"Yes," I said, "but that doesn't mean—"
"Now you replace what you destroyed."
"But where can I get a body?"
Primavera smiled, showing his teeth—both of them.
"I'm sure you can find one, a smart man like you."

HONOR
THY
GODFATHER

Thomas P. Mulkeen

STEIN AND DAY/*Publishers*/New York

FIRST STEIN AND DAY PAPERBACK EDITION 1984
Honor Thy Godfather was first published in hardcover
by Stein and Day/*Publishers* in 1973.
Copyright © 1972 by Thomas P. Mulkeen
All rights reserved, Stein and Day, Incorporated
Designed by David Miller
Printed in the United States of America
STEIN AND DAY/*Publishers*
Scarborough House
Briarcliff Manor, N.Y. 10510
ISBN 0-8128-8107-9

1

Fortunately, he hadn't been a big man.

About 150 pounds on a small and compact frame. This was important. It would make it easier to get rid of the body.

Not that it would be easy.

I'd already whisked him into the bathroom that was part of my office suite. Here he rested in the old-fashioned bathtub with the ugly legs. As for the small spot of blood on the office rug, well, anything I could find I dumped on it—ink eradicator, ammonia, peroxide, mouthwash, Dry Liqueur—and now there was only a wet area about eight inches square. Let the lab men try to find some hemoglobin in that.

It was still lunch hour. The shot must have sounded just as the noon whistles were sending the typists from the adjacent offices out to eat. They were still eating. When they returned they'd pass the *CLOSED* sign now hanging on my door. Ah, but I'd be in here, seated at the desk, trying desperately to think.

It's hard to think with a body in your bathtub.

Sure, I could have called the cops and pleaded self-defense. I could still do it, simply by dialing 911. But this would lead to further complications. You see, I didn't have a permit for the thirty-two. If I dialed 911, this would be my last day in the detective business.

Next question. How was I going to dispose of this body? Should I dump it or destroy it?

Well, it would be nice to believe that my answer was based on logic, but it wasn't. It was based on emotion—on suspicion, maybe hatred. I was thinking about Mrs. DiMaio and how she'd roped me in. And the worst thing about it was that I'd seen the plot dozens of times on TV, everyone has:

A chump who wants to pick up some extra money.

An after-hours job for an attractive woman.

I'll do it, the chump says.

She'd come into my office about two months before and said she had a problem. Seems she was estranged from her husband only he wouldn't admit it. To make him cease and desist, she'd obtained a restraining order from Judge Horowitz. No good. Her husband was still after her. All she wanted me to do was to escort her to a show or something occasionally.

"Don't you have men friends who could take you out?"

"Them! They're all chicken."

"You mean they're afraid of your husband?"

"Yes."

"Is he such a rough customer?"

"I don't know—he's a wild man, a nut."

It hadn't sounded like a very good job, but all businesses are alike: a few get the gravy and the rest have to take the garbage. Besides, she was a nice-looking woman, about thirty-five, quite tall, solidly built, and she'd been smart enough to dye her dark hair auburn rather than blonde. Sticking closely to the script, I took the job.

I liked most of the shows we saw and no husband had ever bothered us. Then today, just half an hour ago, this guy turns up, accuses me of alienating his wife's affections, and comes at me with a switchblade. I pull the trigger and here I am.

I'm getting more suspicious by the minute. Maybe they couldn't agree on a divorce because she wanted custody of the money. If so, then what did she have to lose if he attacked me? More important, what did she stand to gain?

Outside the frosted glass of my waiting room there was a sudden bustle, some laughter, and the tapping of heels. The secretaries were returning from lunch. Their noise made me hear again the background noises: the traffic in the street below, the ticking of my clock. It was twelve forty-two.

Was there really a dead body in the bathtub?

I got up to make sure. Yes, there was.

There was only one answer. Whether Mrs. DiMaio had set me up I didn't know, but if she had, then I certainly didn't want her to collect the insurance or whatever else was coming. I'd have to destroy this body. No body, no proof of death, no death certificate.

The insurance companies don't pay if there's no death certificate.

Getting his head off was the only difficult part. I had the feeling that his brown eyes were looking at me and I felt lousy, but not for long. After all, he'd come after me with a switchblade. Suppose he'd slashed me in the throat or cut the tendons in my right hand? No, he'd been a nut. Only a nut keeps coming when someone points a gun at him and says, "Get back," loud and clear. Only a nut would fight over a woman in the first place—there's enough for everybody.

The arms were easier. I washed most of the blood down the drain. The pipes made a snarling noise like those at home, fortunately not quite so loud.

The afternoon was further along now. As the sun dropped lower, the taller buildings began to stretch their shadows across the smaller ones, such as mine, and it was a time of day I don't like. I have a thing about tall buildings when the light starts to fade. But that's another story.

My phone was ringing.

It kept ringing. I put it in a desk drawer and a few

minutes later, when it rang again, the noise was muffled, less insistent. Outside, the sun was lower still. Long fingers of light were probing into the room showing up all the dust in the air. I stepped to the window and adjusted the Venetian blinds. Then, back to my desk for some more waiting, wishing it were five. The office workers would take off like so many little birds and soon afterward, when it got a bit darker, it would be my time to leave—that pause in the day's occupation that is known as the Children's Hour.

Yes, I'm a college man.

Five thirty-three.

It was fairly dark now, a brave November evening, the kind of night when you'd like to be walking through the wind with some gorgeous woman on your arm. Instead, my arm held a big canvas shopping bag, and the celery protruding from the top of it was strictly for camouflage.

Stopping at a service station, I said I wanted to buy a heavy-duty battery.

"Where's your car?" the attendant asked.

"Home."

"Don't you want a trade-in on the old battery?"

He asked a lot of unnecessary questions. I don't like these guys who are too helpful. Finally, though, he poured the electrolyte into the thing and I put it in the shopping bag with some cans of oil and stuff, covering all my purchases with the celery.

"You like celery?" he asked.

"Can't get enough of it."

I made it back to the office in no time. DiMaio was still in the bathtub. My hands were a bit unsteady as I removed the six caps from the battery and tilted it over him. The acid dribbled out.

Almost at once the skin turned yellow wherever the acid hit, and there was the faintest hissing sound and some white vapor. The skin seemed to soften into putty just before the little holes appeared. I kept pouring until the battery was empty. Then I went into my office and lit a cigarette.

But five minutes later when I went back for a look, I was disappointed. The acid had done only a fair job. Well, I'd known it wasn't going to be easy. In any case, it was time for me to go home.

DiMaio's overcoat was too small for me, but I managed to squirm into it before I put on my own. The rest of his clothes went into the shopping bag with the head and arms. But something had changed.

The arms.

When I took them off they'd been loose and floppy, still warm. Now they were stiff and no longer straight. They felt cold and hard and powerful. It was almost as if they had a life of their own.

Our apartment is on the first floor. We moved down from the third after Mother had the stroke. I found her in bed looking at the Japanese portable TV. While the set looks tiny next to Mother's 190 pounds, I don't want to give the impression that Mother is fat. She's just big, big all over except for her left arm and leg. She has gray hair and wrinkles, a small nose with red marks on each side where her glasses slide down, and false teeth which she wears only on social occasions.

Mother is very smart. Above all, I have respect for her brain. She's not dead weight. Sure, she gets eighty dollars a month from Social Security, but I don't keep her around just for that.

I lifted her into the wheelchair and brought her out to the big easy chair in the living room. When the TV was adjusted right I made her a Rusty Nail—that's Scotch and Drambuie on the rocks—and she asked what we were having for dinner.

"I thought I'd make the short-order special."

"Again?"

"Well, it's late."

But a few minutes later, as I was opening some cans of chicken à la king in the kitchen, she called out:

"Clem, don't you think I should take vitamin pills?"

"Yes."

I was too busy with my other problem to resent her insinuation. It so happened that I used to know a guy named Werner in the funeral business, and I'd remembered that a crematory used a much hotter flame than the one in our oven, and it still took them an hour and a half to burn a body. There was no time to lose.

Turning on the oven full blast, I put in the head and arms on some big strips of aluminum foil. *Arms and the man*, I found myself quoting. *Arms and the man, I sing.*

Tonight I made the short-order special in four minutes flat, using the double-boiler technique that I've devised. But as I came with Mother's tray, she asked:

"What's burning out there?"

"Nothing. I'm just cooking something for myself."

"It's burning, whatever it is."

I was beginning to get worried. Mother would soon realize that I was changing our Friday-night routine.

Let me explain. Living with Mother exposes me to a lot of kidding, but I don't care. I have only one mother and she's not going to be pushed around in some nursing home. At the same time, it's hard for me to keep up with the housework, so I usually let everything go until Friday night.

Friday night is cleanup night. After dinner Mother watches TV while I tackle the chores. Hour after hour the water runs, the pipes in the kitchen and bathroom snarl and rumble, the other tenants complain to the super, but what can I do? Anyway, the racket doesn't bother Mother as she sits there watching the old-time movies. She likes the old-time actors, especially William Powell. She likes him because he's suave.

In any case, this Friday was going to be different and Mother is hard to fool. And so, a little later when I went in with her dessert and coffee, I asked if she wanted a cordial. She said yes, of course, and I put a few drops of chloral hydrate in it, feeling guilty because there was a picture on the Late Show with William Powell and Hedy Lamarr. But even as I was adding the drops, again she yelled from the living room:

"Clem, what are you burning out there?"

About half an hour later I looked in the oven and the blast of heat that hit me in the face took my breath away. Six hundred degrees Fahrenheit! It was as hot as hell. Blue jets of flame, each more than an inch long, were beating down like a battery of blowtorches and white bone was now visible. Still, it would take a while longer, so I went to my room to wait.

Our place isn't large, only four rooms, and much of it is given over to Mother and her nursing gear. Therefore, my bedroom doubles as a sort of den for me. Here I have a second telephone, an easy chair, and my books and stuff.

Sitting there in the easy chair I looked around the room. On the walls were the brightly colored travel posters that the girl from American Express had given me—Monte Carlo and Naples and Aruba and Trinidad. Then there was my bed and my bookcase and the portable cedar clothes closet. I hadn't looked into that closet in years.

A clothes closet is like a graveyard. Here we file away our old dead selves, our life-styles that have gone out of style. Sometimes, looking at the old uniforms and costumes and formal wear, we feel sad or uncomfortable. Oh, my God, did I wear that? And my closet was the worst. It contained as weird a rack of outfits as you can imagine. The bulletproof vest Mother bought me when I first went into the detective business. Dad's ancient tuxedo that I hadn't worn lately. The frogman suit. The fur coat I picked up four years ago when a guy pulled up in a car and offered it for $250. He said it was mink and I'd always believed it. I was going to give it to the girl at American Express but we broke up . . .

Anyway, this room was my den and my sanctuary, the old me and the present me. Right now the present me was sitting in the same easy chair I'd been sitting in for almost twenty years. I took a deep breath. Twenty years and a room full of junk and you might say it's too late.

But it wasn't.

There were other rooms in the city, worse than this. Thousands of rooms in which old men piled old newspapers up to the ceilings. Even now, at this very minute, the newspapers were piling up, and that was the sign that it was too late. Once you start piling up old newspapers, you've had it.

With a start I awoke from my reverie. An odor of burning filled the apartment. I'd forgotten that I left someone in the oven.

Lights covered the city. The city is New York, of course. Young couples were moving through the cold streets, out on the town. It was Friday night, remember. Payday.

I made it back to the office without trouble. The shopping bag was lighter because all it contained was the powdery chunks of bone that I'd retrieved from the oven. They were still as hot as hell—I could feel their heat through the canvas. Only one chunk was missing: a fragment of jaw now safely hidden in my apartment.

It had occurred to me that perhaps it wasn't advisable to destroy the body completely. I ought to save some of the teeth—filled ones—so that they could be identified later. You never know. I might have to account for DiMaio someday.

I entered my office and moved through darkness to the bathroom. The body was still there. Switching on the small night-light, I turned to the cans of oil and stuff that I'd bought earlier.

Whether any of this stuff is good for a car I don't know, but it does burn. When I poured some on him and lit it, a low bluish flame enveloped the carcass and it looked like a miracle or something—a headless shape outlined by blue fire.

The flame didn't last long, so I had to add more fuel. Kneeling there I became absorbed in the game, almost hypnotized. Little bubbles formed here and there in the tissues although the body did not actually ignite. But when all the cans of lubricant were empty I had to admit to myself that I'd just been stalling. Sure, the acid and the flames could do lots of damage, but if I really wanted to get rid of this body I'd have to roll up my sleeves.

It was too late to call the cops. Not with that thing in the bathtub.

The next hour or so was marked by the sounds of water, an interminable roaring sound, a sound like Niagara that seemed to fill my ears and get louder and louder, relentless and never-ending, so loud that others must have heard it too. I had to use the other fixtures in the bathroom. Yes, it was disgusting, revolting, anything you want to call it, but what else could I do?

I jackknifed the remains together and crammed them into the shopping bag on top of the fragments from the oven. Now he was packaged and ready to go but, make no mistake about it, getting rid of a body this way is mighty hard work.

There were a few disguises in the office. A dark-blue peajacket and a knitted cap made me look like a sailor or longshoreman—or so I thought. Slinging the shopping bag over my shoulder I went out and found a taxi to take me to Pier 23.

The pier was alive with lights and workers. Turning left, I walked along the bulwark, looking for a favorable spot.

The waterfront is a dismal place at night. Your feet bang along over old paving blocks and cobblestones, relics of the past, but above you is the modern hum of traffic on the West Side Highway, an elevated structure supported by miles and miles of dirty old steel pillars. Water, cloudy and polluted like stale pea soup, washes against the piers.

I kept walking.

Somewhere out on the North River a foghorn sounded.

13

A blind fog was groping its way in over the bulwarks, a hesitant fog, coming in on little rat feet. I kept walking and, between Piers 22 and 21, I found a dark stretch of water. My pace slowed. I looked around.

Nobody.

Moving to the bulwark, I heaved the package. A gray splash, almost noiseless, and it was gone. I turned away, knowing the water was at least twelve feet deep at this point. Besides, there had to be some white critters in the mud on the bottom. If all went well—

"Hey, you."

A shaggy figure was leaning against one of the steel pillars that support the highway.

"Yeah?"

"Just a second."

He came weaving toward me out of the shadows. Wisps of white fog, curling about his ears, made him look a hundred years old. Just another wino, one of the derelicts who hang around the piers.

I met him halfway. Close up, his face looked like an armpit.

"You threw something in there . . . "

"That's right."

"What was it?"

"A body."

2

I wasn't good for much that weekend. I'd never killed anyone before, not even accidentally, and it really is the way the books describe it. You feel like there's some stain on you that you can never wash off, and you keep holding up your hands and staring at the twelve fingers.

Just the same, I knew I wasn't to blame. He'd come at me with a switchblade. I'd warned him to keep back. And as for the way in which I'd disposed of the body, well, it had to be done that way. But I wasn't a ghoul or a maniac. I've always been basically normal. Take the way I handled the guy at the pier:

He was a witness—the only witness against me—and if I were a maniac I'd have thrown him in the river after DiMaio. But instead I play it cool. I give him the change-up, the switcheroo. I tell him I threw a body in and, naturally, he doesn't believe me.

See what I mean?

Nothing happened that weekend. The cops didn't come and there were no private inquiries. But on Monday night Mrs. DiMaio phoned to ask me if I'd seen her husband. When I said no, she told me that he'd disappeared.

"Is that so?"

"Yes. Some business associates of his told me."

"You said he was in the funeral business?"

"Yes."

"What chapel is it?"

"Scatologgia."

"Aaaaaaaaaaah! Now you tell me."

I was impressed. The Scataloggia Funeral Home was a monument in our neighborhood. Some people referred to it as the Celestial Villa. It was down on Concourse Square near the courthouse and the YMCA.

"Do you know who really owns it?" she asked.

"No."

"The mob."

Then she said that the boys had been asking about me.

The phone rang the next morning as I was preparing breakfast. A deep voice asked for Mr. Talbot.

"Speaking."

"This is Mr. Gilbert. I wanna see you about a case."

"What kind of a case?"

"A missing person."

I told him I'd be in my office at one.

There were three of them. The one calling himself Mr. Gilbert upstaged the others by taking off his overcoat to expose a beautiful gray sharkskin suit with a carnation in the lapel. He was a husky guy in his late forties with wavy iron-gray hair that stunk of pomade.

The others kept their coats on. One was a big moon-faced *paisan* who looked like the village idiot gone to fat. The other, tall and pasty-faced with pale eyes that moved shiftily behind his tinted glasses, was a real natural for the funeral business. Their names were Gino and Karl.

We all sat down.

"You probably guessed who we are," Gilbert began smoothly—a man of the underworld.

I nodded.

"It's this way," he said. "I'm the manager of the funeral home and I sent Mr. DiMaio to pick up some important property last Friday, but he disappeared and so did the property."

"Why come to me?"

"Because he left early that day and told Gino here he was gonna stop off somewhere first to see someone who'd been runnin' around with his wife. So, we talked to Mrs. DiMaio and she fingered you, and we think he came here."

I nodded again, stalling for time. But then Gilbert leaned forward and said:

"Now, you get this straight, boy. There's a lot at stake and we're not kiddin'. You tell us the truth and you'll be all right, but if you try to curve-ball us, your ass is sunk—get it?"

"Sure."

"Okay," he said, as if something had been settled, "now for the first question: Did DiMaio come here last Friday?"

"Yes."

"What did he want?"

"His wife. He told me to stay away from her."

"Anything else?"

"No."

"Did you make any deal with him?"

"No."

"He just left?"

"Yes."

"Did he say where he was goin'?"

"Not a word."

"What time did he leave?"

"It was late."

"How late?"

"Quite late."

"After two o'clock?"

"Yes."

"After three o'clock?"

"I think so."

"Did you lend him your car?"

"I don't have a car."

Gilbert frowned. He looked at the others but they just stared back at him without comment. I figured that they were stooges, here only to show that he had the manpower. On their own they probably couldn't even get themselves arrested. They seemed disinterested when Gilbert told me that I was in bad trouble.

"Why should I be in trouble?" I asked.

"Because DiMaio's station wagon was just hauled away by the cops. It's been parked near here for the past couple of days. And because he was supposed to pick up somethin' worth a fortune at one o'clock last Friday. Now you sit there and tell me that you and him spent the afternoon here havin' a cozy little chat. Now, you can see that you're in a funny position, boy—am I right or wrong?"

"You're right."

"Okay. Then let's have the real story."

I hesitated, glancing at Gino and Karl, and Gilbert caught my drift. A sidewise motion of his head banished them beyond the frosted glass of my office door. Then I asked:

"You said I'd be all right if I told the truth?"

"On my mother's grave." He made the sign of the cross.

"DiMaio's dead."

"What happened?"

"He came at me with a knife and I shot him."

Gilbert was shaking his head from side to side like a bewildered bull. He asked where the body was.

"In the river."

"He always was a crackpot," Gilbert said, making a noise with his lips.

"I couldn't help it. He came at me with a knife."

"You'll have to tell this to the big man."

The car waiting downstairs was a dark-green sedan, nondescript, almost stodgy. The four of us piled in. The driver was a skinny man with a receding forehead who looked like an oversized jockey. His name was Andy. As he eased the car into traffic, I asked our destination.

"Upstate," Gilbert said.

Once on the highway the driver came to life and so did

the car. I felt the thrust of the running gear and noted that there was a floor gear shift. The sedan rushed along, passing Cadillacs as if they were covered wagons and scaring the hell out of me.

I knew the road well, having trailed couples to motels along here more times than I cared to remember. What worried me was that there were a lot of hills and curves farther up. Would this maniac slow down?

He did—to about sixty-five—as we hit the first curve. It bent to the left but, terrified, unbelieving, I saw him turn the steering wheel to the right.

At the same time he stabbed at the brake and we were skidding, to the left. But he just crunched the transmission into a lower gear and stepped on the gas. The car fishtailed, straightened out, and rocketed out of the curve at seventy— eighty—ninety miles an hour.

The deep breath I took was audible throughout the car. Gilbert chuckled. "Kinda gets you the first time he does it."

"Ask him not to do it again."

"Just once more," Andy pleaded.

"Andy used to be a racin' driver. He goes nuts drivin' hearses all the time—you know how it is. That was what he calls the power slide. All right, Andy, but just once. We don't want to frighten Mr. Talbot."

A minute later we were plunging toward the metal barrier at the edge of a cliff, and the white houses in the valley below were tiny and unreal. But then I felt that sickening skid and the sedan careened broadside to the left and I shouted:

"Okay! That's enough!"

We took it easy after that and soon turned off on a country road, passing through wooded areas where the ground was dotted with brown and yellow leaves. The crunch of gravel. The driveway was as long as a football field, our goal a stone mansion between two huge Chinese-looking trees. On the lawn a white-haired man and some small children were playing with a St. Bernard.

We parked and went inside. A butler took our coats. His

nose was very scarred as if it had been bitten off and sewn on again. I looked around at the high ceiling, the black marble floor, the fancy woodwork along the walls, and the fireplace with all those shiny copper gadgets. It was real class.

Andy, Gino, and Karl stood there like the Three Racketeers as Gilbert ushered me into a small library and closed the heavy wooden sliding doors. In leather chairs we waited for the big man.

About five minutes later someone was fumbling weakly at the doors, unable to open them. Gilbert jumped up to admit the man with the white hair.

He was a small man, quite frail, with yellow wrinkled skin. Little simian eyes peered at me through thick lenses. I figured him for seventy, maybe eighty. His name was Mr. Primavera and I knew I'd seen it in the newspapers. The first five minutes were spent in polite inquiries about Gilbert's family.

"How are the children?"

"Fine. The boys are big now."

"How old are they?"

"Rocco is twenty-four. He's finishing college next year. He wants to go to medical school."

"Wonderful! And the other boy?"

"John wants to go to West Point, but I dunno. He's not the student Rocco is. Maybe he'll change his mind."

"Sure, sure. The boy has lots of time."

Mr. Primavera had a pleasing continental accent. They went on talking, ignoring me completely, and I was reassured. These men were okay, and they didn't seem hostile to me. I'd always felt that the Syndicate wasn't all bad because it did give the second generation a chance to compete on an equal basis. Let's face it, by the time they got to this country others had already grabbed the land, the oil, the timber and anything else that wasn't nailed down.

Gilbert was now returning the compliment by asking

about Mr. Primavera's descendants, including the St. Bernard. With a shy smile, the old man said:

"The children asked their grandpa to get them the biggest dog in the world. I couldn't say no."

"There is a taller dog," I volunteered.

Mr. Primavera looked at me. His wrinkled face was angry, hurt. "The man said it was the biggest dog in the world."

"It's the heaviest, but the Irish wolfhound is taller."

"Where do you buy them?"

The interruption caused them to get down to business. First Gilbert outlined the situation. Then I told it my way, omitting the gamy details. The white-haired man listened in silence, but small monkey eyes were studying my face. When I'd finished, the room was very quiet. Gilbert was twiddling his thumbs.

"Infamita!"

A lot more Italian words followed, but the real talking was being done by hand. Mr. Primavera's claw like hands were monopolizing the conversation.

The hand that rocked the cradle. The hands of toil. The firm hand. The helping hand. The hands across the sea. The Black Hand. The warning finger. The accusing finger. Thumbs down—

I didn't like the turn the conversation was taking.

Gilbert frowned at me. "He says you made him look like a sucker. You shouldn't have destroyed that body. Everyone's gonna think DiMaio escaped with something."

"I'm sorry."

"You oughta be. He says he don't see how the organization is gonna save its face."

"But I didn't know."

By this time Mr. Primavera seemed to have calmed down. He even smiled a little, showing his teeth—both of them. In English he asked me if there was any way I could prove DiMaio was dead.

"Yes. I saved his teeth—a piece of his jaw."

"What does this prove?"

"It proves it's him. His dentist could tell."

Mr. Primavera turned to Gilbert and raised his eyebrows. Gilbert said that it would be easy to check.

The old man nodded and said he had to think a minute. He turned his chair around so that he was facing the bookshelves. The back of his neck was very wrinkled. I saw him touch the tips of his fingers together. Gilbert caught my eye and gave me a wink.

I liked Gilbert.

After a few minutes Mr. Primavera turned around again and said he was going to tell me the full story. It seemed that a lot of European countries required that every dead person be autopsied. These laws applied even to tourists. After the autopsy a tourist could be embalmed and shipped home in a sealed coffin. Did I understand so far?

Yes. Well, that's what had happened in the present case. An American tourist died abroad. An autopsy was done. Something was placed inside the body before it was sewn up. The body was flown across the ocean and Mr. DiMaio was supposed to claim it at the airport. Instead, Mr. DiMaio disappeared and so did the coffin.

"You're missing two bodies," I said brightly.

"That's exactly it, Mr. Talbot, and you are to blame. You kept DiMaio from going to the airport."

"But he had no reason to come after me. I never touched his wife."

"Ah, we have a saying in Italian for a case like this . . . how does it go? . . . I cannot remember . . . "

"DiMaio was to blame also," Gilbert broke in.

"Yes. Of course. He failed the organization. That is why we must make an example of him."

"But how can you?" I asked.

"By bringing both of those bodies back."

His words hit me between the eyes. It hadn't occurred

to me until then that this shriveled-up old guy could be off his rocker. But I began to change my mind as he outlined his plan:

First, we were not to tell anyone—not even Andy and the others—that DiMaio was dead.

Second, Mrs. DiMaio would notify the police that her husband was missing.

Third, in about two weeks a body would be found in a stolen car. It would be badly burned but the teeth would identify it as DiMaio. The news would go around that someone who failed the organization had been punished.

"It's not a bad idea," I said.

"Thank you, Mr. Talbot," the old man said.

"I'll be glad to bring you the teeth."

"No, Mr. Talbot."

"I don't understand."

"You will furnish the body in the burned car, Mr. Talbot."

"But where can I get a body?"

"I'm sure you can find one, a smart man like you."

"But it's too big a job for me and it's not fair—"

"You destroyed the body of DiMaio, didn't you?"

"Yes, but that doesn't mean—"

"Now you replace what you have destroyed."

I was about to tell him to take a flying jump until I happened to glance at Gilbert, sitting there stoically, and saw him—ever so gently—shaking his head.

Andy took it easy on the way back, not that it mattered in the frame of mind I was in. What was happening? A few weeks ago I was feeling sorry for myself because of the crummy jobs I got. Now I was in the big leagues. The mob seemed to think I was under an obligation to them and, since I couldn't pay it off, I'd have to work it off.

But one thing puzzled me. What had the funeral home done when it came time for the funeral of the body stolen at the airport?

Gilbert chuckled when I asked him.

"That was easy," he said. "We told the family it would have to be a closed casket. There was no viewin' of the body."

"They agreed?"

"Yeah. No sweat. Oh, the brother gave me an argument but I talked him out of it. You know, they don't embalm bodies in Europe as good as they do here. They shoot them full of Chianti wine or some other stuff and, half the time when we get a body from the old country, it's gone bad and we can't display it. I told the brother he'd never forgive me if I let him look at it."

"But what about a death certificate?"

"No sweat. There's a simple way to put a government stamp on any document. You gotta have a document made out of good paper, of course. You put a half dollar under it and start poundin' away with a hammer and, before you know it, you got a nice circle stamped on the paper with an eagle inside it and, Christ, it looks like the Declaration of Independence."

3

Two days later. I hadn't found a body yet. As I walked the streets I saw thousands of them, all shapes and sizes, many of them more dead than alive, of no possible use to themselves or anyone else, and yet I couldn't get one.

I'd been racking my brain to find a way. The morgues, the medical schools, the hospitals, the crematories, the burial grounds. If I only knew someone in the right place—somebody who'd come through for me.

Just one body. Was that asking so much?

Desperate ideas were thrusting themselves at me, each wilder than the one before. A trip to Louisiana, for example, where cemeteries were said to keep the bodies above ground. A visit to the morgue where I might claim the body of my long-lost brother, Horatio Talbot. I might even have gone off Pier 21 after DiMaio except that I'd left the scuba gear in my other suit.

Under the circumstances I was finding it hard to relax. Even when I thumbed through a magazine the ads seemed to be needling me. *Let Me Prove to You in Ten Days that I Can Give You a New Body. Trade in your old body for a new one.*

Now you may think that my story is a lot of bunk, that a situation like this couldn't happen. You're especially apt to think this if you're from some little town in Kansas where they have elm-shaded streets and county fairs and stuff like that. But with all due respect—and I'm not trying to be a wise guy—I tell you that you're wrong. You don't know the city.

There are all kinds of foreign settlements here, all kinds of splinter groups from the Orient and the Caribbean and the Middle East. Lots of things have always gone on here. I can take you to a museum where you'll see skulls with hatchets embedded in them—relics of the tong wars in Chinatown during the last century.

And lots of things are still going on. Voodoo, puberty rites, vendettas, mutilations, ancient superstitions, harems, white slavery, all kinds of bizarre crimes. Compared with what these other characters do, the mob is pretty mild.

But the mob does have its own primitive code and standards and one thing they won't tolerate is a welsher. I owed them a body, I'd promised to get one, I'd have to keep my word.

Finally I got a brainstorm, a really ingenious idea guaranteed to solve my problem easily and simply. I figured out that it might be easier to get hold of a skeleton than a fresh body. Suppose I went to a surgical supply house and said that I was Dr. Talbot?

One skeleton.

DiMaio's teeth.

Some animal flesh and organs.

A gasoline fire.

Put them all together and you'd have charred DiMaio.

A great idea and, make no mistake about it, twenty years ago it would have worked. It fell through when I learned that there was now such a shortage of authentic skeletons that the med schools were using plastic ones.

In the meantime I'd had to turn down a couple of lucrative investigative jobs, and I'd soon be feeling a financial pinch. It was obvious, too, that I wasn't fooling Mother. She knew that something was wrong. It's hard to fool a woman, especially one who has nothing to do all day but sit around and watch and compare.

26

Even my love life, such as it was, was suffering. There was a new waitress at the Rump and Romp, a restaurant where I occasionally went to get away from my own cooking. She was a big blonde, over thirty but still solid, even taller than Mrs. DiMaio. Her name was Helen. We'd exchanged a few jokes and I'd been thinking of asking her out.

There were a few potential rivals at the Rump and Romp, mostly older men who lived dangerously by eating there all the time. Most of them didn't worry me. Only one of her other admirers looked like competition. This guy was old and he wasn't handsome or anything, but his face had some character or distinction to it. On Madison Avenue they'd call him a type.

Thinning blond and gray hair slicked straight back. A thin nose. Narrow eyes the color of bourbon or Scotch. A stiff military mustache and a general air of horniness like the men they used to have in *Esquire* magazine.

All he needed was a pith helmet to pass for old Abercrombie, the Englishman who went wrong in the tropics.

Too bad about old Abercrombie . . .

He was always watching Helen, following her with those ancient lion eyes as she moved around the place with her swinging stride. She talked to him a lot. He seemed to have a smooth line. There was no doubt that he looked more sophisticated than I did. My face has been compared to a handful of flesh that someone threw against a wall.

I wondered if she went out with him.

She probably did.

I dropped into the restaurant on the third day of my search. It was almost a surprise to see Helen again. I'd all but forgotten about her during my recent difficulties.

My reply to her opening remark must have been a bit absentminded, I guess, because a while later I became aware that I was brooding over some mystery meat while she stared at me from another corner of the establishment. I watched dully as she walked over and poised a pencil above her order pad.

"Anything else I can do for you?"

27

The words seemed to come from the ceiling. I was slow to answer, and she added:

"I thought you liked me."

"I do. I'd like to go out with you but I've been tied up in my work."

"What is your work?"

"Private investigator."

"Oh, cut it out."

When I showed her my identification, she shook her head. "I never would have believed it."

"What did you take me for?"

"Oh . . . a funeral director."

I did a double take. Then I began laughing. She said it wasn't that funny.

"Private joke."

Later, after she brought me some almond cake that tasted like Paris green, I said maybe we could go out for a moonburn in a week or two. She made a face. But they say that any approach will work.

My rival, the guy with the military mustache, had been watching all this out of the corner of his eye. He didn't seem pleased. On my way out I asked the cashier about him.

She said he was a retired undertaker, name of Clive Andresen.

4

I was awake although I didn't want to be. Darkness filled the bedroom and it was warm under the covers. I didn't want to leave my dream.

But something was hitting my right hand. There it was again! I twisted over in bed and fumbled for the switch on the lamp. Whiteness flashed before I saw the red. There was blood all over my hand.

DiMaio's blood.

My mind must have wavered there for a moment because I couldn't move, couldn't do anything. But then there was another soft plop and a new spot appeared on the sheet. Above me the ceiling showed a round red stain. Someone upstairs had to be dead.

What day was today?

Monday. Of course, it would be Monday. It's always Monday when they find you dead.

It makes sense when you think about it. Monday you're supposed to show up for work. Monday people miss you. Monday they come looking for you. And Monday they find you—dead.

I washed up, dressed myself, and tiptoed out past the deep breathing in Mother's room. All I knew about the tenant above me was that he was a young guy named Reynolds with a puppy that barked now and then. I roused Cermak the super and together we climbed the stairs to apartment 2D.

The place was laid out differently than mine, with the kitchen right over my bedroom. We found Reynolds face down on the tattered linoleum with a pool of blood around his head.

A few cockroaches were on the body. This was a good sign—it meant there weren't any maggots. Cockroaches are afraid of maggots and it's hard to figure out why. Why should cockroaches, fast and armor-plated as they are, be afraid of those white blind things? Anyway, the cause of death seemed obvious. A leather belt encircled the left arm and a hypodermic syringe was on the kitchen table.

Cermak was bug-eyed. His stiff Middle European mustache quivered as he asked:

"Is it murder?"

"No. An overdose."

"But the blood?"

"Doesn't mean anything. The body is decomposing. The tissues in the nose and throat always break down first."

"I call the police."

As he went to the phone I heard a slight noise in the room. Very faint. Cermak stopped and asked me what it was.

"I don't know."

I looked around the kitchen but saw nothing. Meanwhile he was dialing hastily. Wrong number. He tried again.

Grabbing the body by the feet, I dragged it across the linoleum. The dead face traced some crude markings, like a kid's finger-painting, in the red stuff. But now I saw the source of the noise we'd heard—it was the puppy, which had been lying under the dead man, crushed by his fall.

It made a little bleating sound. It couldn't move its hind legs.

"Hurry, please," Cermak called into the phone.

While waiting we looked around the apartment. It was furnished in Modern Degenerate and I'd seen it a hundred times before—a big plum-colored rug, psychedelic light clusters, peace posters, paintings of accusing eyes that stared off into limitless vistas, a life-size snapshot of six nude bodies lying prone on a bed with their fleshy rear ends hanging out, a screened-off cubicle where stolen traffic arrows pointed upward, a cellophane-covered jar in which a fly was buzzing around a Venus's-flytrap . . .

But there was stuff here I hadn't seen before, a large collection of little pots and containers, most of them filled with moss and dried twigs and lacquered flowers and berries, all very artsy-craftsy.

"Young people today," Cermak grunted.

As we went back to the kitchen, the doorbell rang. Instead of the cops I confronted a big well-dressed man with a mustache. I'd say he was close to fifty. Backing up a bit, he asked what I was doing there.

"There's been an accident."

He introduced himself as Dr. Hendriques and said he'd been treating Reynolds for drug addiction.

I already knew Dr. Hendriques by reputation. His base of operations was a two-story building he owned down by the courthouse. Here he had lawyers, bail bondsmen, labor unions, and insurance companies for tenants. Most of them were also clients because he testified in court, either side, anytime.

He was also the doctor for the prison under the courthouse and here, so the rumor went, he'd loosened up some of the young punks in the neighborhood who thought they were tough.

Now he came into the apartment and asked to see the body. His dark eyes roved around the kitchen as if looking for something. He seemed to be doing some fast thinking.

We went into the next room and I asked him what Reynolds had done for a living.

"This is it—all this junk you see here. Every spring he went out into the country and collected wildflowers and brought them back here and dried them. Then he'd go to the beach and get driftwood and shells and make this junk.

The florists were always glad to buy what he made. The Japs couldn't do any better."

The doctor spoke almost absentmindedly, all the while looking about the room. But now a muscle in his jaw twitched and suddenly he was standing taller and speaking in a stern voice:

"I'm Dr. Hendriques. I have to look through the rest of this apartment."

Cermak and I didn't try to stop him. He poked around the bedroom, pulled out dresser drawers and rummaged through cabinets and closets. Next he searched the bathroom. Whatever he was looking for he didn't find, and now he became ugly. Striding into the living room he said:

"There's something missing. How long have you two been here?"

He got more belligerent, threatening. You haven't heard the last of this. You're not going to get away with it. He all but accused us of stealing something.

Before I knew it, I was shouting back at him, and only the arrival of the cops made us cool it. About fifteen minutes later, after one of them took my name for his black leather notebook, I asked to be excused.

Downstairs I changed my bedclothes, hoping to rejoin the dream. But I couldn't make it. I dozed off and then awoke at the sound of more footsteps and voices in the room above. A series of thumps. A harsh laugh. More thumps as though a body was being moved. The footsteps left. Then silence.

Reynolds was on his way.

Suddenly I cursed myself. What the hell was the matter with me? I'd been looking for a body and here one had been handed to me, made to order, and I'd given it away.

What did I want—an engraved invitation?

Dr. Hendriques phoned me later that same morning. This time he sounded oily. So sorry about last night, old chap. Apologize for anything I may have said.

"No harm done."

"Mr. Talbot, something that belongs to me was taken from that apartment. Now, I've learned that you're a detective and that you live there. The other tenants might talk to you more readily than they would to someone else. Why don't you drop over to my office?"

"Well . . . I don't know."

In the end I said I'd come.

There was nothing medical in his office except a large bottle of Alka-Seltzer. Filing cabinets, business machines, law books, ledgers, and group photos took up most of the space. From behind a big desk he said:

"Let me fill you in."

It seems that he'd been treating Reynolds with a drug that was a substitute for heroin. What was missing was a large glass container filled with this substitute drug. It must have been taken on Friday, the day the doctor took off for the weekend. Unable to get more, Reynolds had gone to a pusher and bought a fix that killed him instantly.

"How do you know this?" I asked.

"Because when they took the body away last night, the police found one of those glassine envelopes on the floor."

I shrugged. "So what's the big problem?"

"I'll lay my cards on the table, Talbot. One of the big drug companies is paying me to try this stuff out. It's experimental, of course. Now, I'm the doctor at the prison here, but I can't try it out on the prisoners any more because the Food and Drug Administration is too strict.

"I have to try it out on private patients. Naturally, rather than have these jokers cluttering up my office, it's been easier for me to give each one of them a big supply. Unfortunately, this thing happened and the real point is—I was careless. The company's trademark is on the container."

"Then it's the container you want back—not the drug?"

I guess my question had been tactless. His face was gloomy as he said slowly:

"This is big business, Talbot. Public relations are important. The government is using a substitute drug now. You may have heard of it, a yellow liquid called methadone. My company is looking for a better drug to treat all the addicts in the country. My company is after a government contract. Do I have to draw you a picture?"

His story was plausible enough, but you have to remember that I'm supposed to be a detective. That's why I couldn't help wondering if there was any connection between his container and the thing that the Syndicate had smuggled in with the autopsied tourist.

Do you have any more of those containers here?" I asked.

"Yes."

"Could I see one?"

He opened a cabinet. There were dozens of identical glass jars there, each of which contained a whitish powder. The labels were all the same—a prominent drug manufacturer and a long, long chemical name.

When I told Dr. Hendriques that I didn't want to look for the stolen container, his features slackened and his mustache seemed to be just pasted on.

5

A phone call from Gilbert. How was I making out?

"Not too good," I said.

"Why don't you come over to the chapel tonight?"

"What for?"

"Just to talk things over."

I was curious, to tell the truth. The Scatologgia Funeral Home held a kind of significance for me.

Once, years before, I'd been on the fifth floor of the courthouse—some misdemeanor or other—and I'd looked down over my neighborhood. The small one-family houses and the shabby apartments seemed to be hemmed in by the taller buildings that fronted on Concourse Square. Our little streets were clumped together, closed off, and I could see little figures moving about. It struck me that none of them, including me, could ever get out. Oh, we'd move around in there, sometimes kicking up a fuss, but sooner or later each one of us would have to go to his prescribed destination: the courthouse, the prison under it, the hospital, the YMCA with the ex-cons, or the glittering finality of the Scatologgia Funeral Home.

I suppose it was morbid. And ever since that day at the courthouse window, I'd tried to laugh away my fear of the funeral home. Sometimes I thought of it as the Last Motel.

Tonight I found it brightly lit up. Huge stainless steel girders ran up three stories, supporting the glass facade. You could see the metal staircase zigzagging behind the glass, and the people on the staircase looked like manikins in the windows of a fancy store. A moon-faced guy—Gino—stood outside the entrance in a formal black suit.

Nodding hello, I passed into the main reception room where modernistic armchairs and sofas were parked haphazardly across an expanse of red wall-to-wall carpeting that must have cost a fortune. Colored lights played on tubs of green shrubbery along the side walls. There was a tall silver fountain with jets of water that arched gently before tumbling down from tier to tier in front of a hand-painted mural of the Bay of Naples—here the top of Mount Vesuvius was covered with gobs of pink lava that looked like bubble gum.

Not too many mourners were around. I spotted Gilbert sitting behind a desk at the far end of the room in an office enclosed by glass thick enough to deflect a torpedo. He waved at me. I went in and took a seat.

"How's the boy?" he asked.

"So-so."

"Did you get a body yet?"

"No."

"What's the matter with you? You've had five days."

"Speak for yourself."

"Don't you compare my job with yours," he said.

"Why not?"

"I gotta find a stolen body. You can get any old body."

"It's still not easy."

Italian funeral homes are theatrical. There's often a large blue cardboard clock set over the coffin, the cardboard hands pointing to the time of death, three-fifteen, eleven-thirty, or what have you. The bodies are usually exposed to their full lengths because the older Italians are suspicious of hospitals—if they see a relative laid out in half-casket, they think an amputation is being concealed. And in such an atmosphere, the mourners seldom pull any punches.

36

"Oh, John! How you could do it?" came a high-pitched shriek from outside Gilbert's office. He made a face and suggested we take a tour.

The first stop was a chapel off the main reception room. The man in the coffin had no visitors but was surrounded by large floral wreaths. Cautioning me not to laugh, Gilbert pointed out a card attached to one of them.

YOUR UNION BROTHERS OF
LOCAL NO. 377 A.F.L.-C.I.O.
wish you a
SPEEDY RECOVERY

Next we took a service elevator to the third floor, where there was a display of coffins of all types and sizes. Some of the mahogany models listed for thousands of dollars. Gilbert said that the average coffin was twenty-seven inches wide. A cheap one might be only twenty-two inches. Then there were other sizes, first extra and second extra, for really big people.

Gilbert showed me the five or six unoccupied chapels on the second floor before we went back to his office. But the tour wasn't over because a door in the back of the office led to an alleyway between the funeral home and a private house. The alley was shielded above by one of those brightly colored plastic awnings. Another door opened off the alley into an embalming room. A man's body, a white sheet wrapped around the loins, lay on a porcelain table. He looked like a fallen warrior, the illusion aided and abetted by a rack of gleaming lances on the nearby wall.

They weren't lances, of course, but trocars—long hollow metal tubes used to drain and replace body fluids. In answer to my question, Gilbert said that the average body took about two gallons of solution. It was usually pumped in at a pressure of five pounds per square inch, although the pump could deliver about thirty p.s.i., enough to inflate an auto tire.

The rest of the room held a sink, an instrument cabinet, and so on, but what really got me was the array of before-and-after photographs on the walls. Mangled faces gazed into mine. There were deep lacerations running across eyes and noses, mouths that had been ripped apart, ears that were hanging off. Yet the adjacent photos showed these faces restored almost to normal, although heavily coated with cosmetics.

"Who does this work?" I asked.

"Karl did most of it. He's good with car accidents."

"It's like plastic surgery."

"That's right and it's the only job he could do here."

"How come?"

"I can't let him meet the relatives—he scares the piss outa people. You've seen him."

"Yes."

A minute later the door opened and Karl came in. I hoped he hadn't heard us. The white surgical gown accentuated his pallor. You wouldn't want to see that face every morning across your bowl of Wheaties. I was glad to get out of there, back to the office, where Gilbert broke out a bottle and some glasses. The brandy was really good stuff. But just as I was beginning to enjoy my visit, he said:

"How about givin' me some help?"

"What do you mean?"

"Help me find my body."

"I can't even find one for myself."

"Come on. You're a detective. Go to the airport and see what you can find out."

"Have you been there?" I asked.

"Yes. I didn't get nowhere."

"How was the body taken?"

"Easy. A guy drives up in a station wagon. He seems to know his way around. He breaks the seal on the coffin and takes the papers to Customs. He's got an affidavit from another funeral home. No sweat. They put the coffin in his wagon and he drives off."

"So what could I find out there?"

"I dunno. Maybe nothin'. But you could try. You might get an idea for me. I'll pay whatever you want."

"No. I can guess what was sewn up in that body. I don't want to be an accessory."

"Look, I'm not askin' you to get the shipment back, just to find the coffin."

"No dice."

Gilbert held up a hand and told me not to make my mind up so quick. He asked me to think it over.

We dropped the subject. For want of a new topic I asked him if he knew Clive Andresen.

"Of course. Everybody knows him. He's the greatest embalmer in the world."

"Better than Karl?"

"Sure." He snorted. "I'm not saying Karl isn't good, but when you want a big job done right, you call Clive Andresen. I'll never forget how he came through for us, five or six years ago, when the hearse gets hit by a truck on the Brooklyn-Queens Expressway and catches on fire. We pulled the body out somehow, but it was all burned.

"The family goes nuts. They want to start all over again with the body laid out and everything. They was payin' top dollar so we had to go along with it. We call Clive Andresen and he works for ten hours straight. I still don't know how he did it. I know he used parts of a dummy from a clothin' store. It don't matter—he did it. He's the greatest."

6

A November gale was whipping through the streets as I walked home from the chapel. Scraps of paper whirled about in the air like giant butterflies. If winter comes—

It had come. Soon the nights would be freezing cold as the temperature dropped into the twenties and below. Then we'd get the snow, the white blindness of it, and the slush and the traffic jams. Abandoned autos—their owners trudging off into a swirl of blinding white. Abandoned vehicles—just hulks against the snow. Winter scene. The retreat from Moscow.

Fighting the gale I bent forward like a big question mark.

Then the idea hit me. It was so simple! I saw how easy it would be to get a body. All I had to do was rent a car and cruise around the Skid Row areas until I found an exposure victim, some poor derelict who'd expired, a *corpus derelicti*, so to speak. And the beauty of it was that I wouldn't be hurting anybody.

I rented a car the very next day. A black Ford with snow tires and an LSD.

LSD meant limited-slip differential, a mechanical device that's supposed to give you better traction on the rear wheels. I was all set. I had a plan, a car, and the will to win.

That first night was the hardest. I dawdled around home until about nine o'clock. Then I told Mother that I had to go out on a divorce case.

"I thought you'd given up that business?"

"This one pays especially well."

As you've probably guessed, I ended up down by the waterfront. My snow tires revolved slowly over the paving blocks, my low-beam headlights searched the darkness. I was looking for someone. Anyone.

There were men there, all right, half hidden among the girders, the parked trucks, the bales, and the crates, men whose bearded faces blinked and pleaded. Some of them were wrapped in yesterday's headlines. Some of the hands clutched small bottles bearing the red and white label of Twister, a wine they don't advertise on television. Sometimes a rotting mouth spewed curses as I drove away. I didn't really expect to find an exposure victim that first night and I didn't.

The following night, Thursday, was more of the same. This time I combed the Brooklyn waterfront near the old Navy Yard and it's a rough place, believe me. If you ever get a flat tire here—just keep going. But something did happen that second night. You might say I got religion.

Sure, most of these men were too far gone for help. Just the same, there might be one guy I could salvage, just one, if I could only find him. And that's how I got confused there for a few days and lost sight of my purpose. The figure of the *corpus derelicti* became blurred in my mind, and sometimes he was two men rather than one.

Most of the time he was just a poor slob, a loser with dead fishy eyes, and I was going to wait until he froze to death so I could use his body for my own unholy purposes. But then he'd suddenly change into someone else, a bearded Christ figure, struggling under a cross, my brother and my neighbor and my comrade—I was going to lift him up and help him. Anyway, for a few days there while the attack of religion lasted, I drove around automatically, uncertain and troubled, thinking about this man and wondering what I ought to do.

But I never doubted that I'd find him. He was here in the city right now, still alive, still breathing like the rest of us, and he was waiting for me. Somewhere in the black bowels of an alley or a cellar he shivered, knowing that I was near. And some night soon, when the snow was hard and icy against the pavement and the wind rattled the metal grilles and padlocks on the storefronts, we'd have our rendezvous. He didn't know me, but I knew him. I'd know him anywhere.

After a few days of soul searching I was myself again, whatever that meant. I decided to stick to the original plan. But then another unexpected development occurred and I saw that my scheme had one built-in flaw.

The weather.

The weather in New York City is manic-depressive. It's unpredictable, subject to quirks and rapid changes. Many people like it that way, of course, because they feel it makes life here more interesting. Women like it because it gives them an excuse to buy all kinds of clothes. Be that as it may, this was no time for an Indian summer.

I awoke one morning to find old people out sunning themselves on the sidewalk. Kids were rolling hoops and skipping rope. April in Paris, in living color. At 3 p.m. the mercury reached sixty-four degrees, a record, and everywhere the happy, bloblike faces were saying what a beautiful day it was.

Drop dead.

I walked like a sourpuss through the sun-drenched streets, smiling back grimly at people I knew. They didn't understand that my plans were being ruined. How was I going to succeed in weather like this?

I wasn't.

As the fine weather continued I realized I'd never get a body on schedule. The two weeks allotted by Mr. Primavera were almost up. I needed an extension of the time limit. Maybe Gilbert would put in a good word for me.

But I hesitated to ask him because I'd turned down his

request for help in tracing the other body, the one stolen at the airport. All he'd wanted me to do was make a few inquiries. Too bad I hadn't—

It wasn't too late. I could still do it without letting Gilbert know of my belated change of heart. The first step would be to get the name of the deceased from the obituary column of some old newspaper.

The obituary column of the *Daily News* is known as the Italian sports page. It listed the name of a man who had allegedly been buried from the Scatologgia Funeral Home at the time in question. He must be the one.

Lo Curto was his name. Sebastian J. Lo Curto.

A sunny November afternoon found me driving out to Kennedy International Airport. I parked near the TWA building. Wrong building. I had to trek over to the section for international arrivals. Referred from one guy to another, I ended up with an old fellow in stained work clothes and slipped him five bucks.

"I have to see your identification," he said.

His lips moved as he memorized the card.

"A coffin came in from Europe about two weeks ago," I said. "It was Friday, November the fifth. Do you—"

"You mean Flight 307. Everybody and his brother's been askin' about it. Come out the back."

We went out on the field. Despite the bright sunshine, the wind came on strong across the concrete runways. Yellow trucks were circling a huge plane. We walked toward a metal warehouse.

"What happened?" I asked.

"It was routine. A guy came here in a station wagon. He had the right papers, far as I could see. He signed for the coffin and took it away. And don't ask me what he looked like because he was disguised."

"What do you mean?"

"Just what I said. He was disguised. He had a big red wig on. He had dark glasses and his hat was pulled down. You couldn't see his face."

"Why did you give him the coffin, then?"

"Wasn't any of my business. He had the right papers and he signed for it."

"What did he sign?"

"The bill of ladin'."

"Could I see it?"

"Sure."

We reached the warehouse and went inside. Bales and packages of all sizes were piled around us. A hairy creature was grunting in a cage. In a small office a kid snoozed at a desk. The old attendant moved to a filing cabinet and got a small piece of paper.

There was a signature at the bottom that I couldn't make out. It could have been anything from Garfinkel to Garibaldi. With my little camera, the one with the wide-angle lens, I snapped a picture of the bill of lading as the attendant's mouth fell open:

"What's the idea? You're makin' a big case outa this."

"No, it's really nothing. What happened was that the relatives hired two different undertakers, and now one of them is trying to prove that the other took the body without authority. You know how they are."

"Yeah." He sounded doubtful.

"Do you remember anything else unusual about this man?" I asked.

"No. Just the wig. It was a humdinger. He was big, too, as I remember and he wasn't so young, but he wasn't old. Wait—there was something else. He was a lousy driver. He banged his car into the building."

"Show me."

We walked to the big metal door. It had some deep scratches on it, about a foot off the ground, and dark-blue paint was ground into them. I collected some of the paint particles in an envelope and drove home.

But the clues weren't much good. The puzzling thing was the wig, so obviously a phony that even this old codger had spotted it immediately. I couldn't figure it. Why would the thief wear such an outlandish disguise?

Unless it was a double bluff. Unless the thief had natural red hair.

That night I went to the funeral home to ingratiate myself with Gilbert. What happened to me there should happen to all apple polishers. Before I so much as opened my mouth, he told me he was in bad trouble. James Lo Curto, the brother of the stolen man, was putting the pressure on him.

"How?" I asked.

"He came here. He's a lawyer, you know. He said he was suspicious when I didn't let him look in the coffin we buried from here. Then he found out that DiMaio disappeared on the same day. He hints that DiMaio could be in the coffin."

"Is he serious?"

"Naw. That's just an excuse. But he knows somethin'. He wants to shake me down. He said something about diggin' up the body."

"An exhumation order?"

"Yeah."

Gilbert looked kind of harassed. Above the pin-stripe suit and the red carnation his face was older.

"I wish I'd known this," I said. "I went out to the airport today."

"Yeah? Did you find out anything?"

"No. But the guy there memorized my I.D. card."

"So what?"

"Now I'm mixed up with two bodies."

7

The exhumation was a big success.

City officials and official witnesses crowded around as the coffin of Sebastian J. Lo Curto was hauled out of the grave. Then the coffin was opened. Inside they found eleven gray cinder blocks wrapped in old army blankets and a section of red carpeting.

Gilbert was arrested.

His arraignment in court was the signal for Judge Joshua Horowitz, a real actor, to play up to the reporters. Denouncing the cruel and dastardly nature of the crime, he ordered Gilbert held for the grand jury. Bail was quickly posted, however, and following Gilbert's release I went to see him at the funeral home.

It was the first time I'd seen him in a really bad humor. He looked shabby and there was no carnation in his lapel.

"This guy Lo Curto is burned up," he said. "He's gonna bring a civil suit against the chapel for one million bucks."

I whistled.

"Yeah, we got trouble." His eyes focused on me absently. "How you makin' out—as if I gave a good goddamn."

"I came here to get my story straight."

"What story?"

"The one I tell when they ask what I was doing at the airport."

"That's easy. Just go along with my story. Me, I find a

sealed coffin here so I bury it. How did I know that DiMaio had stolen the body? Later on I hired you to find DiMaio, and you went to the airport looking for *him*—get it?"

"Yes. That's what I'll say."

Just then there was a knock on the wooden door that led to the alley. Karl came in, his pale face worried, and said they had a slight problem.

"What?" Gilbert snapped.

"Maybe I should speak to you outside."

"No. We got no secrets here. You got a problem— problem four hundred ninety-seven—let's have it."

The embalmer hesitated, looking meaningly at me, but Gilbert rapped impatiently on the desk. Finally Karl said:

"Well, we brought one in an hour ago and I started working on him now and I think—I'm not sure—he could be alive."

"Think? Don't you know? Where's the death certificate?"

"We don't have it. The doc won't be back till tomorrow."

"Haven't I told you guys a million times not to do that?"

Karl was silent, gazing at the floor. Gilbert got to his feet and told me to come along. In the embalming room Gino and an older man were watching the nude body on the porcelain table. It was the body of an old man with the words IT'S ALL YOURS, BABY tatooed on his organs of generation. Karl pointed out a small incision in the armpit area. What looked like fresh blood was trickling from it.

"Who's got a mirror?" Gilbert called.

They tried all the usual methods, holding a mirror to the mouth to see if it clouded, feeling for a pulse in the temple—

"Take him back," Gilbert ordered.

"But, boss—"

"Take him back. It's about time you guys learned a lesson. I dunno if this guy is alive or not, but don't bring

47

him or anybody else here any more without a death certificate—get it?"

Gilbert and I went back to the office, where he poured out two big shots of brandy. We touched glasses. He began telling me about some of his other problems in the funeral business. Seems the pastor of a local church had been giving him a hard time.

"Every time he announces a death from the altar, he gives the cause of death, no matter what it is. 'So-and-so died Tuesday from an overdose of sleepin' pills,' he'll say. 'On Friday Mrs. Nancy Umbriago passed away from cancer of the sex glands.' He tells the congregation everything: abortions, TB, gonorrhea, diarrhea, he don't care. Then the relatives blame me for it."

"What does he have against you?"

"I dunno, but it could be because he caught Gino stealin' blank baptism certificates from the rectory. You see, a good friend of mine had some kids he wanted to deduct from his income tax—"

Gilbert stopped abruptly. His eyes were staring over my shoulder toward the outside entrance.

A police car was parked there. A group of men in plain clothes got out. I recognized the elderly attendant from the airport. There was another man, big and dignified in a black overcoat and a gray homburg, who looked like a wheel.

"That's Lo Curto," Gilbert said.

A minute later the group entered the funeral home. One man detached himself and came at us over the red carpet. Once inside the office he identified himself as Lieutenant Pytlak, local precinct.

Gilbert was indignant. "What right have you guys to come here?"

"Now, take it easy. I think you ought to cooperate."

"Cooperate my ass! You got a hell of a nerve bustin' in here. I haven't been convicted yet. Where's your search warrant?"

"Look, Mr. Gilbert." The detective was almost whispering. "This guy has friends among the brass. He's been breaking our chops. We have to go along with him. He wants this man from the airport to have a look at everyone who works here."

"To hell with him."

"Why don't you make it easy on yourself? We thought it would be easier to have a lineup here. Otherwise we'll have to bring everybody down to the station. Let's satisfy this guy. Get him off your back and off ours."

"What do you think I'm runnin' here—a police academy?"

"Just play along," the detective said.

Gilbert sighed. He looked at me. I shrugged. He looked at Pytlak, who nodded encouragingly. Gilbert picked up his phone and pressed a button.

"Andy? It's me. Listen, some of the boys are out runnin' an errand. The minute they get back I want everybody up here in my office. Everybody—understand?"

Pytlak sat down to wait. Outside the main group of invaders stood talking by the front entrance. We had to wait about twenty minutes before the staff appeared. I knew Gino, Karl, and Andy. There was also the older man I'd seen just now in the embalming room, and a young kid, a new apprentice named Cinquegrana. He seemed to think that this lineup idea was groovy.

Italian names are funny. Most of them mean something. Cinquegrana meant "five grains." His ancestors might have been in narcotics.

Anyway, nobody objected to Pytlak's proposal. The boys dispersed to get their hats and coats. When they reassembled, the detective pulled out a paper bag filled with cheap sunglasses. We each donned a pair before lining up in front of the mural of the Bay of Naples.

"All right, Mr. Krell," Pytlak called.

"Just a minute," Gilbert broke in. "Some of you cops get in this lineup! You know that's the way to do it."

Pytlak apologized. He motioned to the group at the door and two dicks came over, put on dark glasses, and stepped in with the suspects.

Now the airport attendant shuffled across the room, looking intimidated. No doubt we seemed like a gang of hoods. He walked slowly down the line. On command each of the suspects spoke a few words. Then the airport man scratched his head.

"Well?" Pytlak demanded.

"I couldn't say."

"Can you identify any of these men?"

"Yes—him." He pointed to me.

"Was he at the airport?"

"Yes."

"Did he take the coffin?"

"No."

"What about the rest of these men?"

"I couldn't say for sure."

Pytlak asked what he meant.

"They all look sorta alike and they don't even have wigs on."

"That's what you think," a detective chuckled until Pytlak's dirty look froze him.

Actually, the old guy was right. The seven men standing there did look alike, even though I knew they had different builds and features.

Now the line broke formation. The sunglasses went back into the paper bag. Pytlak thanked Gilbert for his cooperation. "You're welcome," Gilbert said. But then he took a few steps toward the group waiting at the entrance and shouted:

"You satisfied now, Lo Curto?"

The man in the dignified clothes strode to the center of the room. In a deep voice he said:

"No. My brother's body was stolen and it's too late for you to give it back. Somebody's going to jail if I have to turn over every rock around here."

"Ah, rock this."

The visitors left. In front of the mural the suspects formed a circle, laughing and joking. Gilbert asked Karl if he'd gotten the body back all right.

"Yes and no," the embalmer answered.

"What does that mean?"

"They didn't want him back. So we just dropped him and took off. We left the wagon with the motor running."

"That's the boy. Now you're usin' your brains. All right, you guys. Back to work or whatever you do here."

Gilbert and I went back to his office and finished our brandies. As he reached for the bottle, the phone rang. He picked it up and listened. A change came over his face. More serious. Respectful.

"Yes," Gilbert said finally. "I understand. But I think he's been tryin'—"

Silence again as Gilbert listened some more. I couldn't catch his eye. The person on the other end seemed to be doing a lot of talking.

"Yes, sir, I'll talk to him . . . Yes, I'll tell him . . . but maybe you could make it longer . . . maybe ten days . . ."

Gilbert's voice trailed off. His face was grave as he replaced the receiver. Before saying anything he poured out some more brandy. I noticed that he'd made mine a double. I braced myself for the bad news.

"That was the big man," Gilbert said. "This newspaper publicity has him all upset—all this talk about the empty coffin and me gettin' arrested. It looks like DiMaio got away with something. We gotta save face by showing that he didn't. You gotta get a body."

"I've been working on it. Once the weather turns really cold I'll be able to get lots of them."

"He don't want lots of them. He wants one. He wants you to bring DiMaio back right now."

"How long do I have?"

"A week—no more, no less. A week from the time I give

you the message." Gilbert looked at his ornate gold watch. "It's ten after four. A week from now. I tried to get him to give you ten days, but he don't listen."

I said nothing. We drank our brandy. He offered more but I shook my head and got up to leave. When I was at the door I heard him call:

"Clem."

It was the first time he'd called me by name. It sounded like he wanted to be friendly. I turned around.

"I'm sorry," Gilbert said.

8

The next day was Thanksgiving. I busied myself entertaining Mother. We had one of those TV dinners, turkey and stuff in a tinfoil container that you put in the oven for forty minutes.

It was lousy.

Maybe it wasn't really that bad, but my thoughts were elsewhere. Holiday or no holiday, I had to go out that night and get a body. It was ten o'clock when I started the car and headed for the waterfront.

All day long the weather reports had been good. A cold front was sweeping down from Canada. Icy winds up to thirty miles per hour. Temperatures falling to ten degrees in the suburbs. With luck we might have a blizzard.

At the first red light I opened the glove compartment. DiMaio's teeth grinned back at me as if to say: you are not alone.

The waterfront was deserted. Black hulks moved toward me from all sides—ships, warehouses, trucks, girders, and bales of cargo. Again my tires drummed over the paving blocks with that hollow sound. I caught a whiff of the salt in the air, but then the stronger odors of oil and tar and musty burlap took over. Wind buffeted my side windows as I cruised along slowly, my eyes ranging right and left.

Nothing stirred except some shreds of newspaper in the gutters, driven by the November wind. My car humped along over the cobblestones. A burst of noisy light as I passed a saloon where men staggered out the battered door. But where was *he*? Uptown, downtown, what street, what gutter?

About five minutes must have passed. My car crept along, passing more ships and warehouses, and now I was in an area where boxes and crates were jumbled together in big piles and pyramids. There were markings on the boxes, numbers and letters of the alphabet, and for a second I was a kid again, lost among these building blocks and toy ships, a kid who didn't know what the letters meant, a kid eager to be frightened by a Jack-in-the-box that would spring up with the grin of a dead man.

But none of the boxes opened.

And as I kept going, the toys and boxes disappeared and I was old and shabby and on my own, and I had a job to do and a shabby stinking job it was, at that. A whistle sounded somewhere. A high wall, black with seventy years of soot, was dead ahead, a factory on the outskirts of the waterfront.

Where was *he*?

That dull dead face with the fishy eyes. That wrinkled face and those musty clothes. Those worn-out fingers, already stiffening. The *corpus derelicti*. I'd know him anywhere.

Turning the car around I started back, creeping along, this time on the bulwark side. Now the ships loomed taller, threatening dark masses, black on black, most of them carrying only a few lights. Once more I smelled the salt in the air.

The tires humped grudgingly over the paving blocks, crunching on broken glass. Overhead was the rumble of the traffic that never stopped. Creeping . . . creeping along like a creep . . . a shape on the left . . .

Something was wedged between two bales.

I stopped the car. Its motor was idling rapidly, missing now and then like a frightened heart. My flashlight played on a body that was face down and it was him. A bum in a brown overcoat that was too big for him, a shock of long gray hair. There was no doubt that he was dead. A drunken body retains some shape, a dead one sags all over. Only the dead can really relax and then only for a few short hours. They sag before they stiffen.

It was him, average size, white, maybe fifty or so, just what I needed. Dragging him over to the car, I opened the back door but just then—out of the corner of my eye—I saw the flashing red lights come down the side street.

The cops.

No—it was an ambulance. I'd have to hand the body over to them.

Like hell I would—this body was mine.

I threw him in the back, jumped in myself, and slammed the door. As I clambered over into the front seat I saw that the ambulance had stopped. Its lights were flashing blood-red against the girders. They must have seen what I'd done.

My motor roared hoarsely as I took off, but then I heard the siren. The ambulance was going to follow me. Twin spotlights went on and the glare sprayed off my rear-view mirror in a dazzling halo, blinding me—

I swerved to avoid a truck.

We raced along by the bulwarks. The ambulance was a block behind, hell on wheels with its fiery lights and the shrieks of its siren. The schmuck behind the wheel wanted to be a hero. Once he alerted a police car I'd be done for.

I turned left up a side street, uphill and one-way. The ambulance turned also, but I'd gained more of a lead. I was a block and a half away from him when a distant light turned red. The ambulance could run through all the lights. They were bound to get me. Then I remembered something—a game from my teens.

Swinging up on the sidewalk, I made a U-turn. Now I was coming back down the hill, straight for the ambulance, stepping on my high-beam button, blinding him, blowing my horn. How do you like it, schmuck?

Right at him I came, my lights glaring into his, gambling

that he'd be chicken even though he outweighed me by two to one.

At the last second he gave ground, braking to the side out of my way.

"Chicken," I shouted as I went by, my tires humpitting over the cobblestones, my brakes starting to grab. Slowing at the first corner I made a right and shot off. By the time this chicken turned his heap around, I'd be away.

And so I was, speeding through a red light, turning up a side street, yelling "Chicken" to no one in particular, making a left and slowing down. A few minutes later I pulled over to the curb.

From the floor in back the dead eyes of the body gazed at me. There was a dignity, even a strength, in his features and the lips, now drawing back in the *risus sardonicus*, revealed his perfect teeth. God, was he handsome! Once he must have been somebody—a great lover—the black sheep of a famous family—

Carefully I drew a blanket over him.

The next step was to steal a car. Parking the Hertz rental on a dark street, I set out on foot. A sign said East Seventy-ninth street and I realized I'd come all the way across Manhattan to Yorkville, the German section of the city. I strolled along looking for an old Chevrolet, the easiest car to steal, and at last I found one.

A beat-up convertible with Sunkist written all over it. Fix-or-repair daily. But there was no reason for me to burn up a good car. Besides, the gas gauge in this heap registered half full.

I turned on the ignition with my small screwdriver. The motor blustered. But my search had taken me quite a few blocks out of the way and, as I drove back, some one-way streets and a few traffic lights held me up. When I finally spotted the Hertz car it was pulling away from the curb. A car thief was gunning it down the street—

That's where I made my first tactical mistake by racing

after it, blowing my horn. This just made the thief panic and he barreled through a couple of red lights and I had to follow. A flash of reality told me why.

The teeth.

That fragment of jawbone in the glove compartment of the Hertz car was the only thing that could identify the man I'd killed.

This was what was running through my mind as I followed the black car through the streets of the city. *The teeth.* I kept on his tail, hoping to cut him off, but the old convertible wasn't up to it. He turned left at Ninety-sixth and headed crosstown toward the West Side.

The lights were with him. He didn't have to run through any more signals. He just breezed through and so did I. On the West Side he turned up the ramp that led uptown past Riverside Drive to the upstate highways. The electric signs on the Jersey shore blazed brightly. Reaching the bridge that spans the Harlem River, he slowed up at the automatic toll taker and motioned toward the basket. A light turned green. He shot through the gate as I braked, fumbling for a dime. My throw was high, wide and hasty. The coin bounced out of the basket.

No time to waste.

I gunned past the red light and an alarm went off. The noise faded as I kept going. Now the toll gate vanished from my rear-view mirror. Ahead were the parkway and the red taillights of the Hertz car. The convertible was laboring heavily, but I told it: don't quit now. A series of backfires was its answer.

The Hertz car wasn't going too fast. Once I found that I could keep up with him, I was able to relax a bit. I'd remembered that there wasn't too much gas in the Hertz car. It was just a question of time before he ran out. Then I'd catch him and I was going to beat his ears off—

This pipe dream didn't last long. The Hertz car suddenly picked up speed. The thief must have looked at the fuel gauge and realized that he had to make his move. He was going to lose me if he could. I pressed on the accelerator to keep up with him, but my heap was now shuddering along at seventy . . . seventy-five, and it wouldn't take us long to reach the mountain curves through which Andy had taken me on the power slide.

Seventy-five . . . eighty . . . fast as the old car could go. It shook as if it were breaking the sound barrier. My hands were numb on the wheel. Just a few miles more. If I kept after this slob, he might try to take those curves at a high speed—

But what else could I do? *The teeth.* The body I might be willing to write off, but not the teeth. I couldn't let him go.

I tried to signal him with my horn. Since I didn't know the S.O.S. of the Morse code, I tried to play it by ear, tried to make it sound like the wireless in that movie about the *Titanic*.

It didn't sound too good.

But I kept at it, though, and then I tried flashing my headlights off and on to warn him. If he noticed me, he paid no attention and the two cars were going up a long grade now, climbing steadily higher into the hills, and I knew we were coming to the first curve. Once again I tapped out the S.O.S. with the horn.

Too late.

The black sedan swept into the left-hand curve. Both hands gripping the wheel, I braked to forty-five and saw the flash of red as his brake lights flared. That's when he lost it.

A shriek from his tires. A tremendous crash as the Ford slammed into the guard rail and teetered on the edge of the slope. Then silence as I stopped about a hundred feet past him and ran back to the wreck.

Flames were eating at the crumpled front end. One of the wheels fell off—I heard it tumbling down the mountain. Somehow the courtesy lights went on when I wrenched open the front door. Blood had spattered the dashboard.

The driver was jackknifed forward. A blue eye looked at me from the flattened thing that had been his head. The blue eye was now close to an ear: a Picasso painting in the flesh. Some pink stuff ran down near the ear and the hair above was gray, an old man's hair. But in the back of the car the body of the *corpus derelicti* was intact, still under the blanket.

I reached for the glove compartment.

The car moved. It lurched a fraction more past the shattered guard rail as I jumped back. My hands were shaking—I'd almost gone over with it. It certainly wouldn't support my weight. To get the teeth I'd have to lean my weight on the car, swaying there in the wind like a crippled bug.

I guess this was what they call the moment of truth.

I looked around for something, anything, maybe a fallen branch, something I could use to open the glove compartment. There was nothing there. It was dark on the mountain and all I could see was the far-off lights of approaching cars. They were miles off, sure, but it wouldn't take them long to reach us. I only had a few minutes.

One of them went by.

I was still standing there. Flames were edging their way under the car towards the gas tank. There was still time to get the teeth if I was fast enough, agile enough, if I could throw myself backward as the car went over.

Another minute went by. The headlights below were closer now. It was still possible to do it. Fred Astaire could have done it. One of those Russian ballet dancers could have done it easily. Maybe I could do it if I had the guts.

Another minute was gone.

And then I admitted to myself that I wasn't going to try. I couldn't reach out for those teeth, even though they were little more than an arm's length away. But if I couldn't get them, neither could I let them be found here at the scene.

So I got in back of the car and pushed. It moved. I

pushed again and there was a grinding of metal as the car broke through the guard rail, shuddered like a live thing and plunged down the mountain. I heard the explosion as I ran back to the Chevy. Had to get out of there fast.

9

The suspense was getting me.

Two whole days had passed since the wreck and still no word from anyone. The lab men must be cutting into the corpses now, delving into the blackened sweet-smelling flesh in an effort to identify the two victims. But that was their problem. My concern was with the teeth. DiMaio's teeth.

Had some eager beaver found that piece of jawbone in my car?

No wonder I was sleeping poorly. My dreams were filled with faces that grinned, the way they do when a guy is really screwed and can't fight back.

Sunday came and went.

Then Monday.

Tuesday.

On Wednesday I got a phone call from the Missing Persons Bureau. They asked me to drop over the following afternoon. I said okay, wondering if they'd found DiMaio's teeth in my car.

There was a way by which I might find out beforehand. I could call up Mrs. DiMaio and ask her indirectly. You know, subtle-like.

This I did. I got her on the phone and asked about her missing husband and she told me that Missing Persons had contacted her lately. Seems they needed some routine information to complete their records. But she didn't elaborate and I was finally forced to ask point blank if they'd inquired about her husband's dentist.

"Yes. How did you know . . .?"

Her voice trailed off and then returned, now quavery.

"Does that mean he's dead?"

"No, of course not."

Missing Persons is located in an old-fashioned building on the grounds of Bellevue Hospital near East Thirtieth Street. It was originally put there because Bellevue had the biggest and busiest morgue in the city at that time. The next afternoon I took an express subway to Thirty-fourth Street and changed to a local that let me off at Twenty-eighth.

It's a downhill walk to Bellevue Hospital on the East River. As I walked along, the apartment buildings became more dilapidated. So did the people. I was now leaving the American sector. Slogans and obscenities were scrawled on every wall. New York. City of graft and graffiti.

I walked slowly, looking about me eagerly in an attempt to absorb all the sights and sounds and smells of the city. This was corny, I admit, but—who knows?—this could be my last day of freedom. I knew they'd found DiMaio's teeth in my car.

In a musty room papered with yellowing photographs and circulars, some men were seated around a wooden table. Perched at a nearby desk was a horn-rimmed stenotypist. She was small at the top and wide at the bottom—stenographer's spread.

"Take five, Gertrude."

Wordlessly she got up and shuffled out of the room, a crumpled pack of cigarettes in her hand. If this was supposed to convince me that we were talking off the record, it didn't work. The detectives pretend to talk friendly to you, man to man, and all the time some guy in the next room is taking it down.

They were asking about my background—probably trying to find out if I had any political pull—when a detective came in who wasn't from Missing Persons. He was from a special squad that keeps tabs on the legitimate operations of the Syndicate, the laundries and restaurants and garages bought with their narcotic profits.

Flannery was his name. He was a big guy, good-looking in a florid kind of way, and he kept smirking at me as I talked to the others. I'd already taken a dislike to him because he wore a Chesterfield coat with a velvet collar. To make it worse, he had a bow tie.

"What about Mrs. DiMaio?" he asked me.

"What about her? She hired me a few months ago when she separated from her husband."

"What did she want from you?"

"Protection. She said he was bothering her."

"Did she ever talk about getting rid of him?"

"No."

"When did you talk to her last?"

"A few days ago."

"Keeping in touch, huh?" Then he added, "Don't try to bull us, Talbot. We know a lot. Every time the mob buries a captain or a soldier we have men at the funeral with their ears open. That's how we find out what's going on."

Gertrude was back now. She sat before the stenotype machine and limbered up her fingers. She took my name, address, and other particulars. Then the official questions began.

"You recently rented a car from the Hertz Company?"

"Yes."

"What happened to it?"

"It was stolen."

"Did you report this to the police?"

"No, only to Hertz."

"Why not?"

"I thought it was up to the owner—the Hertz Company—to report it."

"Did you have any passengers in this car at the time?"

"Yes. One passenger."

63

"And who was that?"

"A Mr. John DiMaio."

Yes, that's what I told them. I knew they'd found DiMaio's teeth in the car. What else could I say under the circumstances?

The rest of my story was short and simple. An anonymous phone call had told me where to find the missing man. I found him. I left him in my car when I went to make a phone call. When I came back, the car was gone. End of story.

Strangely enough, the detectives didn't slap the handcuffs on me. They just looked significantly at each other. Flannery was smirking. I waited while Gertrude typed up the statement. I signed eagerly. For some reason—for the moment, at least—I seemed to be in the clear. But when I asked what progress they were making on the case, one of them snapped:

"We don't have to tell you anything."

"Just asking a simple question."

"And I'm giving you a simple answer: none of your business."

"I cooperated in coming here."

"In a pig's eye you cooperated."

It didn't look like I'd do myself any good by staying there, so I decided to beat it. And despite the *brusquerie* of my dismissal, I felt better than when I'd come. I was still free and, somehow, I seemed to be in the clear. A block or so away I heard my name called. It was Flannery. He joined me and we resumed walking.

"They gave you a hard time," he said.

"Yes."

"Not as hard as they should have. Where'd you dream up that fairy tale?"

"It was the best one I could come up with."

"It stunk."

We walked the next block in silence as I wondered what he was after. Finally I asked:

"What about this DiMaio case? Have they found him?"

He waved a fat finger at me. "Now, now, Talbot. You haven't been entirely frank with us. You can't expect us to tell you things."

"All right." I clammed up again.

But he seemed disappointed by my resignation. He took me by the arm and his eyes were greedy. We slowed up as he said:

"Look, you seem to be a fairly smart guy. I liked the way you handled yourself in there. We ought to get together some time."

"I'll try anything once."

"Good. Where do you usually hang out?"

"Down by the river."

"I know, I know," he said, disgusted. "Drop in any time."

The next four days dragged by like an endless freight train in slow motion. Jumpy as a bedbug, I hung around the apartment, venturing out only to the candy store, where, morning and evening, I was always the first to grab the newspapers and scan all the pages for just one little item.

Goddamn it! Drop the other shoe!

But on Monday night I had the feeling that this was it. There was going to be some news in the papers about the wreck. It was a premonition. So at 9 p.m. I was back at the candy store, pacing about outside, waiting for the delivery truck for the *Daily News* to appear.

I saw two lights far off in the distance.

And then it came, going *ker-plang, ker-plang* over the manhole covers and there was a screech of brakes as it halted to let the guy in back hurl a bundle of the early morning edition to the sidewalk. I ran over and ripped off a copy. My cold fingers turned automatically to page 4 and there it was:

There was only one way to figure it. When I pushed the car over the cliff, somehow the jaw fragment had ended up near the driver, who just happened to be toothless. The crashes, the explosion, and the fire must have messed him up so badly that the lab men had mistakenly assigned the teeth to him—and he became DiMaio II.

Needless to say I didn't attend the funeral nor were the charred fragments buried from the Scatologgia Funeral Home. The La Bomba Funeral Parlor got the job and a toothless car thief was filed away in an expensive coffin.

But—so what?

The case was over. A life for a life. A body for a body. I'd come through for the Syndicate, I'd helped them save face. Everybody ought to be satisfied now except, maybe, Mrs. DiMaio.

Sure enough, just before midnight, she came through with a hysterical phone call.

"You knew my husband was dead when you talked to me. You helped them kill him! His body was found in your car."

"Now, wait a minute—"

"You filthy murderer! You'll burn in hell for this!"

What could I tell her?

Yet the vehemence of her abuse could not dim the glory of that day. At last I'd been successful.

When I was younger I used to think more about success but later, as the drab routine of the city began pressing down on me, I decided to forget about it. About this same time they began showing films about scuba diving on TV.

You know. Coral reefs, exotic fish, Lloyd Bridges, giant clams, clear green water, and the strange creatures that lived at the bottom of the sea. That's when I bought the frogman suit and the scuba gear, hoping to open up a whole new world for myself.

But it's no good around here. The first hundred feet of ocean is like cold you-know-what. You swim out doing the Coney Island crawl, your left arm pushing the garbage away from your face while your right does the dog-paddle. You get out beyond the breakers and find that there's nothing much there.

I did see a sand shark once, a fairly big one, but it sort of shrugged and moved away.

10

When the phone rang the following evening I knew it would be Gilbert. It was. He said he had something for me.

The chapel was brilliantly lighted, but empty. Water still bounced down from the tiers of the silver fountain. Gilbert indicated a white envelope on the desk.

"The big man asked me to give you this."

"I couldn't take anything like that."

"Don't be a chump. You had expenses, didn't you?"

I looked inside the envelope. There seemed to be about ten bills there, all of them hundreds. I put it in my pocket.

"Nice goin' on that body," Gilbert said. "We gotta drink to it."

He poured our some liquor and tried to be festive, but I saw that his heart wasn't in it. He looked tired and downcast although dressed with his usual flair.

There aren't too many ways to hide a dollar. You can eat it or drink it or have a big wardrobe of suits, but that's about all. I felt sorry for Gilbert. When I remarked that business seemed to be bad, he shrugged and said:

"What could you expect? Oh, we'll still get the captains and their relatives, but as far as the local people go—forget it. Only one job last week and it was no good. Just from the name you could tell it was a horseshit case."

"What was the name?"

"Wheeler Bowden."

"That's not an Italian name."

"Naw."

Wheeler Bowden was a straight-outer. Straight from the hospital to the crematory. You can't make any money on a cremation. Now if you got a name like Cosimo Gianfrancola . . .

"Couldn't you cut prices?" I asked.

"Naw. The big man said to stand pat. We're not gonna crawl to nobody. Sooner or later inflation's gonna come and, when the other chapels raise their prices, the people will come back to us. You see how the big man thinks?"

"Yes. He's clever."

"You can say that again. The big man has a brain."

"Unless you wanted to try this new gimmick. You know, cryonics. Freezing a guy and bringing him back to life two hundred years later."

"Yeah, I read about that but it would never work with the Italians. You freeze one, you'd have to freeze the whole family. An Italian wouldn't want to come back if he couldn't have his family with him."

Gilbert lapsed into a moody silence. I couldn't think of anything else to say. Sipping the brandy, I let my eyes roam over the office. It was handsomely furnished. The two walls that weren't glass were paneled in a light wood on which diplomas hung, testimonials to those who'd made the grade in mortuary science. There was also a picture of a hearse with the caption, *Why Walk When You Can Ride?*

"You gotta help me," Gilbert said abruptly. "I got more problems than ever. Now I gotta find the body as well as the shipment."

"Count me out."

"You could make yourself another bundle."

"You don't know what I've been through already."

"You never did tell me what you found out at the airport."

"Nothing much. I got some paint from his car and a sample of his handwriting . . . just a second . . . here."

Fumbling in my pocket I finally came up with the photograph of the bill of lading. Together we examined the signature.

My wide-angle lens had done a good job. The printing on the bill of lading was clear and so was the body snatcher's signature, although way off the dotted line. The first two letters were *G* and *a*, but then it trailed off wavily like a child's drawing of the ocean.

"It's a phony name, of course," I said, "but he may not have been able to disguise his handwriting. You might have a handwriting expert make some comparisons."

Gilbert's stubby fingers had closed over the photo. His face brightened. Here was something he could work on. "Yeah," he said. "I could compare with the people who work here. Trouble is, there's a lot of them. We even have women workin' here."

"Women?"

"Yeah. Hairdressers. They come to fix up the dead women. Hey, what about that? Hairdressers—wigs—the guy had a wig—get it?"

"You're reaching."

There was a large stack of unopened mail in my office. Many of the letters were from industrial firms that were discontinuing my services because I'd been unavailable recently. These letters I resolved to answer at once. Maybe I could woo some of my clients back.

The phone rang.

It was Flannery, the wise-guy detective from the squad that watches over the Syndicate. He said he was coming over to see me. I didn't argue and, big as life, he was in my office forty-five minutes later.

"You got any bugs around here?" was his first question.

"A few."

He stared at me. "I mean tape recorders."

"Oh, no."

"Mind if I take a look?"

"Help yourself."

He looked in my desk drawers, turned over some of the furniture, and examined my filing cabinets. Finally he sat down and lit a cigar.

"Understand you were at the airport a few weeks ago?"

"Yes."

"Looking for this Lo Curto?"

"No—for DiMaio."

"Uh-huh. This was before you got that famous anonymous phone call telling you where to find DiMaio?"

"That's right."

"Have you had any calls telling you where to find Lo Curto?"

"Any day now."

Flannery was puffing on the cigar, studying me calmly. All at once I decided that I had nothing to gain by getting fresh with him. I told him that I honestly didn't know where the body was.

"Uh-huh."

"What's it to you, anyway?"

He knocked some ash from his cigar. "You're an American, Talbot. Doesn't it ever bother you the way these dagos get ahead here?"

"No."

"Well, it bothers me. I'd like to see some of the big money. I been thinking maybe we could join forces."

"How could I help you?"

Before answering me he scratched his head. Some white flakes fell on his suit. He brushed them off and grumbled:

"I got athlete's head. Every time I go to a bar they break the glass afterward . . . Well, what I was getting at is that you always seem to be where the action is. But I've got some connections, too. If we worked together, maybe we could get somewhere. Take this Lo Curto case. There had to be something in that coffin besides a body—"

"Count me out," I said.

"Then there was something else in that coffin?"

"I never said there was."

"Talbot, did you share your toys with the other children when you were a kid?"

"I don't remember."

"I'll bet you didn't. That's the trouble, nobody wants to share with me. Everybody else is getting theirs so, just because I want mine, that doesn't make me a criminal. Besides which, I got a special grudge against funeral homes."

I asked why, and Flannery told this anecdote of his early years:

He was just a rookie cop, a kid with a blue suit and a badge, patrolling a beat near a funeral home. A girl rushes up to say that it's not her father in the casket. He asks her if there were any distinguishing marks and she says yes, an anchor tattooed on the chest.

He goes into the funeral home. There was an anchor but, when he rubbed on it, it came off and the funeral manager falls to his knees, begging for a break.

It seems there had been two bodies, this girl's father and a man about seventy-five. They were supposed to cremate the older man, a German, but instead they burned up this girl's dad.

Then they called in a specialist who dyed the old man's white hair and injected wax into his face to take out the wrinkles. They placed the casket in a very dark corner and everyone was fooled except this one girl.

"Who was this specialist?" I asked, suddenly interested. "Was it Clive Andresen?"

"How did you know?"

"I've heard about him."

"You're like horse manure, Talbot. You're all over the place."

I shrugged.

Now Flannery was cursing the funeral home because they'd only given him a hundred and he'd been too green to ask for more. "The cheap bastards," he said. "They still made a profit on the case. And I could have put them out of

72

business! Taking advantage of me because I was a green kid."

I wondered how I could get rid of him.

"Look," I said, "you're right. There was something in the coffin, probably a shipment of dope or something. But all I know is that nothing's turned up yet. The body hasn't been found and neither has the coffin. If you want my opinion, I think the shipment is still in the coffin."

His face lit up like a pinball machine. This was what he'd been waiting to hear. His voice rose:

"That's it! That's it, Talbot. The guy who stole it is lying low. He's afraid to move it because he knows the mob is watching. He may intend to keep it hidden for years. Don't you get it, Talbot? It's still up for grabs."

"Count me out."

For about five minutes he argued with me as the ash accumulated on his cigar. But I held firm. I wasn't going to get mixed up with any more bodies.

Half an hour later, just as I was making progress with my paperwork, the outer door opened and three men came in. One of them was James Lo Curto, the stuffed shirt who'd promoted the lineup at the funeral home. The two glowering young men with him were strangers. They walked over to my desk without ceremony.

"Come right in," I said.

"I'm James Lo Curto," the lawyer announced in a deep voice. "You've seen me at the funeral home. These are my nephews."

I nodded.

"You phoned me earlier today," he continued.

"There must be some mistake. I've never phoned you."

"I think you did. I recognize your voice."

"Impossible."

He frowned. "Let's start over. You know my brother's body was stolen and I know you're working with the funeral home. Now, I had a phone call today offering to return my brother's body. The voice sounded like yours; at least it didn't sound like an Italian-American, much less an Italian. I still think that you made that call."

"Well, I didn't. Period."

"I have a recording of it," the lawyer said.

"Good. That would prove it wasn't me."

"Why do you say that?"

"The voiceprint. Everybody's voice gives a different pattern when they run it through this electronic gadget they have now. If you don't believe me, I'll let you record my voice so you can make the comparison."

That stopped him for a minute. The two young men were looking at him, waiting for the next move. He still hesitated but then, being a big wheel, he had to have the last word.

"I'm not going to argue the point with you at this time. But you and your employers had better get one thing straight: we're not going to pay ransom to get the body back. Somebody's going to jail."

I shrugged my shoulders.

This made him mad. He said that I was just a little guy without any protection and he knew people in the right places. Did I realize he could take away my license?

"I can't sleep over it."

"Keep it up, schmo—excuse me for calling you by your first name—and you'll be out on the sidewalk, you and that mother of yours."

"Beat it."

The two nephews moved closer, their faces tense. I stood up. My eyes were level with Lo Curto's. More words, more escalation, more threats, and then it happened. One of the nephews lunged forward and grabbed my left arm.

I seized the guy, jerked him off balance, and rushed him against the edge of the nearest pointed object, which happened to be the projecting corner of a filing cabinet. It was a trick I'd used before: there's something about a sharp metal edge going into the back muscles that discourages people.

An agonized groan. His arms relaxed. I threw him to the floor. James Lo Curto was retreating as the other kid bounced a fist off my head. I came backhand at the kid with my right, catching him on the forehead, but I'd forgotten about the graduation ring from Aaron Burr High.

Scalp wounds bleed like hell. Blood streaming into his eyes, he staggered after his uncle, who was now near the door. The third guy joined them. "You'll pay for this," a voice yelled as I herded them out of the office. The typewriter noise from the adjacent suites had stopped as secretaries peered out at us. It was all rather humiliating.

11

Same day, same place, later in the afternoon. I looked out the window of my office. The shadows of the big buildings were starting to reach for me. Time to go home.

I hadn't gotten much work done after the Lo Curtos left. I'd been thinking about the stolen body. Flannery and I had more or less agreed that it wouldn't show up—at least, not for a long time. Now someone was offering to sell it back.

It didn't figure.

In any case, it was no longer any of my business. Count me out, I'd told everybody. Big Clem Talbot isn't getting involved with any more bodies.

My outer door opened. Two men came in. On their faces was that look of honest graft.

"Mr. Clement Talbot?"

"Yes."

"Warrant for your arrest."

"On what charge?"

"Assault with a deadly weapon."

"Oh, is that all?"

They looked at each other. One of them asked what else it could be.

"Nothing. I thought it was something serious."

"It's serious enough. What's your version of it?"

"Self-defense—necessary force."

This last phrase I knew he'd recognize. "Necessary force" is the standard defense against a charge of police brutality.

On the way to the station house they told me that the Lo Curto boys had signed separate complaints alleging that I'd attacked them with a dangerous weapon. They had wounds to prove it.

"They're lying," I said.

"Let's hope you're right. They really came loaded for bear."

"What do you mean?"

"Hell, they had everything. A lawyer—he's their uncle—and a letter from a doctor and a picture of this kid's back where he says you stabbed him. You know, one of those Polaroid snapshots, but in color."

"They didn't lose any time. Who was the doctor?"

"The one who owns that building by the courthouse."

"Hendriques?"

"Yes."

They booked me at the station. The desk man was a friend of mine, but there was nothing he could do. I'd have to go to Night Court. When I phoned the funeral home, Gino said that Gilbert wasn't there.

"Listen," I said. "Do me a favor. Try to get in touch with him and say that I'm in trouble. I'll be in Night Court."

The court wasn't crowded and I soon found myself standing before the judge. He was a homely, cranky-looking mug with a Brooklyn accent, nothing like Judge Hardy in the movies. James Lo Curto was there to testify that he'd witnessed the assault. He and the judge seemed to be buddies. Before I knew it the judge was saying that my case would be held over for the grand jury. In vain I protested that the charge was ridiculous because it had been three against one. His Honor snapped that I was stating a conclusion.

"But, judge, I think it's a reasonable conclusion."

"The law doesn't distinguish between a reasonable conclusion and one that's unreasonable, fella. A conclusion is a conclusion. The fact that two of these men have wounds allows me to conclude that you assaulted them with a weapon."

"But, your honor—"

"Case held over for the Grand Jury. Next."

I'd had it. The entire proceedings had taken less than five minutes. Gilbert wasn't in court and I couldn't make bail. Next thing I knew I was in the prison under the courthouse where again I gave my name, address, and so on. This time they asked me if I used narcotics. I then had to take my clothes off and take a shower with about ten other men. I kept my back to the wall.

We dressed and were led down a corridor. On the way I saw a tall figure in a long white coat. Dr. Hendriques. Our eyes met momentarily but his face remained expressionless. He spoke to one of the guards as the procession halted.

Now another guard was talking to the doctor. I couldn't hear what they were saying. They seemed to be arguing. Finally the second guard said, "If you insist, Doc," and Hendriques left, peeling off his white coat as he strode away.

Our group moved again, now down a long corridor which was strictly institutional. Cold stone and rusting metal and a dull gray paint over everything. Even the faces of the guards seemed covered with gray paint. Naked light bulbs had been screwed into the ceiling and everywhere was this cobwebby dust and a chemical odor. We came to a metal staircase and began climbing, single file.

"Not you," a guard said, holding my arm.

"What is this?"

"Down this way."

He motioned to me to take the down stairway as the last of the other prisoners disappeared. I heard their shoes shuffling away somewhere above us.

I didn't move. "What is this, the dungeon?"

"Maximum security."

"Are you kidding?"

"Move."

I started down the metal stairs. Far below were the echoes of our footsteps. There were no windows on the staircase, just that gray paint over the bricks. I stopped at the first landing but he told me to keep going.

Down another flight. It was colder and damper here, strictly subterranean. Only one small bulb burned in the ceiling. To my right was a cellblock, dark and empty. I saw the handwriting on the wall:

Screw you, it said.

"Who sent me down here?" I asked.

"I don't know."

"It was the doctor, wasn't it?"

"In here." He motioned toward one of the cells. I stepped inside and he slammed the sliding door shut behind me. Turning, I looked through the bars. He fumbled with some keys and I heard a click.

"Gimme your shoelaces, your tie, and your belt."

After I passed the various articles to him, he asked if I'd had supper.

"No."

"It's late but maybe we can rustle up something."

"Thank you."

He left. I heard his feet stomping up the metal stairs. The sounds faded away and suddenly there was a loud silence. In the dim light I looked about my cell. It was about seven by seven. When I stretched my arms overhead I could just about touch the ceiling. That meant it was about eight feet high, and the cell was about the size of a room at the Y. The back wall was solid brick but the sides were vertical metal bars through which you could look into the adjoining cells.

Each cell contained a metal bench, a basin and faucet, and a metal bucket. A strong odor of ammonia hung in the air. Sitting on the bench, I looked out into the corridor. Some time passed. I wondered why Gilbert hadn't been in court.

More time passed. I didn't have a watch. They take that from you so you can't cut your wrist or throat with the crystal. For the first time I felt hungry.

Something moved. I saw it out of the corner of my eye.

A rat. It was a large gray one, moving down the corridor close to the wall outside, stopping now and then, its whiskers moving. It didn't make a sound.

Where had it come from? The walls all seemed to be of brick or stone and there were no holes that I could see. But there had to be holes somewhere. And what would happen when they put out the lights?

Not that there was any reason to be afraid. Rats are slow. That's why you don't really have to be afraid of them. With my size twelve bluchers I could stomp any rat that came into the cell. On the other hand, you don't want to fall asleep when rats are around because they usually go for the face.

A sound of footsteps. The rat disappeared somewhere before another guard arrived with a metal tray. He was an old man, not particularly mean-looking. He handed the food in to me, item by item, spilling some of it in the process because he had to tilt the plates, small as they were.

"Thanks," I said. "Oh, what about the rats?"

"I can't do anything about them."

"Don't they ever use an exterminator?"

"On the other floors."

"But not here?"

He shrugged.

"This cellblock is kept as a reservation for them?"

"I just work here, mac. I get my pension in June."

"I understand. Well, thanks for the food."

After he left I ate some of the food even though it was cold, succotash and strips of fatty bacon and chocolate pudding.

The rat came back, bringing a friend. I didn't try to scare them away. It was psychology: why let them know that I was the one in the trap? A small brownish one joined them. They were all twitching their whiskers.

Sure, it can't happen here. This is the twentieth century, the United States of America, Fun City. They can't do this to us.

Anyway, I'd survive. All it would mean was a night without sleep, hardly the first time. I'd get bail tomorrow. But suppose I was some poor schlumpf who couldn't make bail? Now I knew how they loosened prisoners up.

The rats moved about slowly. They were slow and clumsy. I'd stomp the first one to come into the cell, kick him out into the corridor, and let the others eat him.

When the old guard came back for the dishes, I asked if there were any messages for me.

"No. They close everything up at six."

"Have you got a broom I could chase the rats with?"

"I can't give you nothing. Regulations."

"Then could you leave the lights on all night?"

He shook his head and looked guilty.

Again he left and the rats returned. I could see five now. Luckily for them, they didn't come into my cell. Not that it was their fault if they were hungry. I felt sorry for them, scrounging around down here, but I wouldn't want them as pets. There weren't any white ones. Come to think of it, you never saw white mice, except in captivity.

The lights began to flicker.

They flickered rapidly and grew dim, then flared up weakly to flicker some more on the silent cellblock. It was like one of those old Warner Brothers movies about Sing Sing when Jimmy Cagney was going to the electric chair. But they wouldn't have one here unless Hendriques had built his own—not that I'd put it past him.

After flickering for three or four minutes the lights went out. Blackness now. I curled up on the bench and tried to see out into the corridor. I couldn't see anything. Once in a while there was a scurrying sound that set my imagination working overtime. There could be dozens of them now. I saw them lining up, getting ready to rush me, rows and rows of them with little red eyes, the big gray ones in front, the brown ones hanging back, all of them waiting for the signal.

Jumping up, I kicked at the bars. The noise, heavy and metallic, clanged through the darkness and there was a sound like the surf as they scampered away.

The rest of the night was more of the same. Soft sounds, whispers, very faint at first, then gradually louder as more and more of them gathered, then still louder as they drew nearer. And each time the rustling became real loud I'd jump up and kick at the bars and shout:

"Get out of here, you bastards."

What a sap I'd been to think that I was no longer involved! Boy meets body, boy loses body, boy regains body—I'd thought that was it.

It didn't get too cold in the cell but it was damp. A heavy odor of chemicals came from the metal bucket. The blackness was everywhere and seemed to stretch so far and wide that I had an illusion of space, and I didn't seem to be in a tiny cell.

"Get out of here!"

My shouts were getting louder. I groped around, found the faucet, and drank some of the water.

Time passed, I didn't know how much. No matter how often I chased the rustling sounds away, they came back. And once I caught myself dozing off—I jumped up just in time and splashed tap water on my face and walked about the cell. To sleep, to dream, to wake up with some warm furry little face next to your own. No. Never.

More time had passed. It must be after midnight now. If I counted to thirty-six hundred slowly, it would be an hour. And time is one thing you can depend on. Even men like Hendriques and Lo Curto can't bend it, can't twist it to their own purposes like they twist everything else. Across the ocean the big chronometer at Greenwich, England, was working for me.

"Get out of here!"

Maybe it was three or four in the morning. A new day outside. Thursday, December the ninth. But inside the rustling had started again.

Suddenly the lights went on. The glare made me close my eyes. I felt like hell. After a minute I opened one eye and saw that the rats were still there, but not so many as I'd thought. I chased them away and stretched out on the bench, hoping someone would come with coffee. No one came.

I must have dozed off. When I awoke my right arm was cramped and tingling.

The rats!

I looked out into the corridor. Some of them were at the door of my cell, sticking their whiskery noses through the bars.

12

A bail bondsman got me out at noon. I phoned Mother and found her surprisingly calm. She explained that a Mr. Gilbert had visited her last night.

"Oh? What did he say?"

"He said you were out of town on a job for him."

"Yes, that's right. Hope you weren't worried."

"I don't worry when you're working for someone like him. Such a nice man, and so well dressed! He's certainly an improvement over the bums you used to go with."

"Yes, I know."

"He must be very successful."

"He's a leader in the community."

I slept most of the afternoon, cooked dinner and walked to the funeral home. Again it was brightly lit but empty. Gino, a forlorn sentry, stood at the door. The gaudy decorations and the red carpet looked forlorn also, something like a flashy woman who's been stood up on a date. Even the water from the silver fountain seemed to dribble.

Gilbert and Karl were talking in the glass-enclosed office. Gilbert was the first to see me. He motioned for me to come in. I said I'd wait if they were talking business.

"Business? We got no business. Karl here is tryin' to talk me into takin' on some welfare cases."

"At least we'd look busy," the embalmer said.

"We wouldn't fool nobody. Lemme think it over."

Karl took this as a dismissal. After he left I thanked Gilbert for going to see Mother. He waved my thanks away with a stubby hand and asked me about the jail episode.

The news that someone was trying to sell back the body hit him hard. A look almost of panic in his brown eyes. He asked:

"Why would they want to sell the body to him and not to me?"

"I don't know."

"I gotta do something fast."

He decided to contact Lo Curto and set up a deal. If Lo Curto could get the body back, the funeral home would pay the tab. In return, Lo Curto would drop all charges.

"What about the shipment?" I asked.

"I get that back too if it's still in the body."

"You don't want much."

"Look, I'll pay, I'll pay. I'll pay for the body—the shipment—the coffin—the funeral—I mean both funerals—I'll even pay off the guys you cut if you'll go and talk to him."

"Why should I talk to him?"

"You're an outsider. He's not mad at you."

"Then why did he have me put in jail?"

"Talk to him. Ask him to drop the charges against you. I'll pay for everything. We'll make a package deal. Everybody's happy."

"Count me out."

He argued with me and, finally, somewhat against my better judgment, I agreed to talk to Lo Curto. Maybe I could get him to drop the assault charges. But before I did anything at all—I had to settle up with the doctor.

"Forget about him," Gilbert said.

"I can't forget it."

"You can take care of him later."

"I have to do it now."

"Make a vendetta at this time? I need you now. Help me with this other deal and I'll help you with the doc later."

"No. I have to do it alone."

"But why?"

"This guy thinks he's so big that he can't be touched, but there's nobody that big. All it takes is one man to even the score."

Gilbert gave a long low whistle. He tapped his forehead significantly. Then he stood up and said:

"Let's go."

"You don't have to get involved."

"Yes I do. You need help, boy. I didn't know before that you was a Sicilian."

We went out into the main reception room. Gilbert told Gino to close up in another hour. A gray Cadillac convertible took us two blocks to the building owned by Hendriques. Lights were still on in the doctor's office. At the curb was a white Lincoln that looked like Moby Dick.

We parked across the street and waited. I lit a cigarette. To pass the time, Gilbert told me the story of Clive Andresen and the two floaters.

"These two guys drowned while they was fishin' in Jamaica Bay. They was in bad shape, but he fixed them up with that secret cosmetic of his. Only thing was, he laid one of them out in this brown suit.

"The wives was pals, too, and the first thing they notice is this suit. 'What a beautiful suit Joe has,' one of them says. 'Too bad your Mike couldn't be buried in one like it.' 'Yeah,' the other one says, 'I'm gonna speak to Mr. Andresen.'

"So she asks him, but it was the only one he had.

"Before he knows it, these two dames start cryin' and bawlin' and throwin' their arms around each other 'I want for your Mike to have that suit,' the first one howls. 'No, I wouldn't think of it,' the other broad answers. 'I insist, Mary, I want for Mike to have that suit.' 'No, I won't take it.'

"They go back to Andresen, blubberin' and howlin', and he gives them that smile with his mustache and gets them calmed down. 'You ladies go out for coffee,' he says, 'and by the time you get back everything will be taken care of.'

"That's the way he always worked, smooth and quiet. And don't forget he was all by himself this day—it was a Fourth of July—and you know it takes several guys to dress a stiff—"

I asked Gilbert what happened.

"Nothin'. The women go out, still blubberin' and carryin' on, and they come back fifteen minutes later and it's all done. Mike is wearin' the brown suit."

"But how could Andresen dress him so fast?"

"He didn't," Gilbert said. "He just switched the heads."

Gilbert became silent as the lights in the doctor's office suddenly went out. A few minutes later a tall figure climbed into the Lincoln. We trailed the white car through the dirty streets of the shopping district. Big signs announced fire sales, rummage sales, package sales, bargain sales, and just plain sales. Groups of young punks were kicking discarded crates and cartons into the gutter. We were about a block behind as the Lincoln turned into a residential district. Soon we came to a section where there were mansions and a scattering of high-rising apartment houses. Gilbert slowed up as the car ahead signaled for a right turn.

The Lincoln's headlights flashed on a garage door set in the side of a big apartment house. The door moved up automatically. Down a stone ramp we followed the Lincoln into a dimly lit underground garage. It rolled toward a distant wall.

I heard the garage door closing behind us. As Gilbert maneuvered the Caddy into a vacant spot, my eyes were on the Lincoln. Now it was parked, and its headlights blinked off.

"Remember, this is a cement floor," Gilbert hissed.

Hendriques, big and prosperous-looking in his blue overcoat, was walking past us. I jumped out and slammed a fist into his belly.

"What—?"

His arms were flailing but I was in on him. The boxing writers would have called it a two-fisted body attack. I didn't say a word.

He landed a couple of good ones, and blood trickled into my left eye. We were grunting like pigs. I drove a one-two into his belly and even the heavy layers of the double-breasted coat failed to soften the impact. He couldn't take it in the breadbasket.

"What do you want?" he managed to gasp.

When I didn't answer he caught me in the face and then on the side of the head. He said something else that I didn't hear. His face was a white mask bobbing about in the naked light.

Again he hit me on the side of the head. His lips moved as if he were speaking. Maybe he was. I didn't hear anything. Behind him was the white blankness of the wall, a great picture screen, and I was watching the shadows there.

The shadows were fighting on the wall. They moved back and forth, up and down, now rising and now falling. Sometimes they were towering hunchbacked shapes that swelled up to the ceiling, sometimes they swooped down to the floor. But they kept moving, always moving, and their blows were noiseless and caused no pain.

From time to time a real face floated in to block that whitewashed screen, but the shadows still struggled back and forth beyond the faces, those familiar faces that you'd know anywhere only you were never good with names. One face with a funny mustache that was just pasted on. Another, the face of a friend, I forget your name. An animal look on this second face and great excitement in the eyes. And in the throat below a hoarse wordless cry, cheering someone on . . .

Then through a pinkish haze the shadows were back again, twisting, heaving, dancing, ranging up and down the wall, and one of them was moving faster, striking harder. But the other shadow was big and hunchbacked with arms that flailed like great dark wings sweeping along the white-washed wall.

A face under the lights—a look of desperation—another face—

Now the shadows raged up to the ceiling, and one of them was crouching and cruel. Another flurry of dark wings on the wall. Then a shadow was sinking through the haze and there was only one shadow left.

"Wait," a voice gasped. "I'll tell you."

A man was on the floor. A man stood over him.

"It was DiMaio's idea—"

The man on the floor was talking in short bursts. The other man just stood there, glaring down at him. The man on the floor was a doctor. The other man was named Gilbert.

Nobody paid any attention to me as I stood there panting, winded, too exhausted to think. In boxing a round seems to last forever.

I moved closer to them, remembering now. I was Clem. The doctor saw me coming and cringed a little as if I were going to give him the boot.

"Keep talkin'," Gilbert said.

"Few months ago—asked me if I had connections—I said all kinds—he said he might be able to get hold of some merchandise—said I'd think it over—few weeks later he came again—he said to get ready—I had the idea he was going to hijack something—told him not to bring it to my place—"

"Where was he gonna bring it?" Gilbert asked.

"He never told me—that was the last time I saw Di-Maio—he disappeared—when I heard about the body that was stolen—I knew he must have taken it—and then I read the other day that he was dead—murdered—I knew someone had caught up with him—I've been waiting—waiting for them to come after me—"

"And here we are," Gilbert said.

The rest of the interrogation produced only negative

answers from the doctor. No, he hadn't made a phone call offering to return the body. No, he hadn't discussed the subject with James Lo Curto. No, DiMaio had never said that there was anyone else in on the plot.

Hendriques had recovered his breath by this time. He begged us to give him a break. We let him off with a warning.

Overall, the evening had been a great success. Gilbert was jubilant as he drove me home in the Cadillac. We stopped for a light and he pounded me on the back and said:

"You brought me good luck, boy. I come along for the ride and he thinks the beatin' is my idea."

"You were overdue for some luck," I said.

"You're right and I get the picture now. DiMaio went to your office to set up an alibi. He thought you'd have him arrested while some other guy stole the coffin."

"Don't remind me. I killed him for nothing."

13

The next morning I phoned Lo Curto's office and a girl said he was in court. I found him trying a case on the fourth floor. The courtroom door was padded all over with some heavy brown cloth except for a small diamond-shaped window through which I could see Lo Curto making a point before the judge. Voices came through only faintly. Then another lawyer jumped up and began waving his arms. Above the judge's bench an old clock registered eleven-twenty.

I waited, walking up and down the blank corridors.

When the noon whistles sounded I was back by the padded door as Lo Curto came out with two sharp-looking characters. They were talking earnestly.

"Excuse me," I broke in.

They stopped.

"Something important to discuss with you, Mr. Lo Curto."

"Oh—er, yes. Just wait here a minute for me."

The corridor cleared rapidly and he was back asking what I wanted.

"It's that matter we talked about the other day."

"Yes. Well, why don't we talk about it over lunch."

Downstairs he sort of bundled me into a taxi and we ended up at a dark restaurant a good mile from the courthouse. After steering me to a booth in a far corner, he ordered ham sandwiches and coffee. I noted that the waitress wore a hearing aid.

It figured.

"Well?" he said.

"Mr. Gilbert asked me to talk to you. There's been a new development in this case. We think we know who was responsible for the theft of your brother's body."

"I'm listening."

"It was DiMaio."

"I see."

Lo Curto paused and looked off into space. Well-kept fingernails drummed momentarily on the cream-colored plastic of the table top. His gaze returned to me and he said:

"Inasmuch as DiMaio is dead, that's mighty convenient."

"That doesn't mean that Gilbert is trying to evade the responsibility. He's willing to cooperate with you in any way. If you can buy the coffin back, he'll pick up the tab. He'll pay for everything, including mental suffering. What more can he do?"

Again the well-kept fingers drummed on the table. The lawyer's face was a mask.

"Just what was DiMaio's idea?" he asked.

"Well, as you can probably guess, he thought that something valuable was being smuggled in with the coffin. He thought he could hijack it. He had two accomplices. One was a man with connections who could dispose of the stuff without going through the mob. The other man actually took the coffin and hid it while DiMaio was elsewhere setting up an alibi.

"But something went wrong. DiMaio disappeared and the whole plan was screwed up because he'd been too cute to tell either of his accomplices who the other one was—"

I stopped talking as our sandwiches and coffee arrived. The waitress shuffled over to another table to fetch a jar of mustard.

"Anyway," I said when she left, "the guy who took the coffin was left high and dry. All he could do was wait. But he finally learned last week that DiMaio was dead. Now the stuff was all his, only he didn't know how to market it. He didn't dare try to sell it back to the mob. He gets the idea of selling the body back to the family—that's you. So he calls you on the phone."

Lo Curto didn't say anything. He'd taken a bite of his sandwich while I was talking. His brown eyes were almost blank. I wondered what he knew that I didn't. He had me at a disadvantage. Taking my cue from him, I bit into my sandwich.

"Is what you're saying fact or theory?" he asked at last.

"A little of each."

"You seem to be implying that there's some illegal merchandise in the coffin with my brother. Don't you realize that I can't be a party to anything that's illegal?"

"Wait—I never said that there was anything in the coffin. I said that DiMaio thought so. It's all—hearsay."

This last word was one he could appreciate. He nodded, his eyes narrowing. But it was high time that he told me something.

"Have you had any more phone calls about the body?" I asked.

"No."

"Didn't he say he'd call again?"

"Yes, but he hasn't so far. Now that brings up another point: what does Mr. Gilbert propose to do if this person doesn't contact me again?"

I shrugged. "I suppose he might try to find out who this caller is. It may be easier now that we know that DiMaio was in back of it all. For one thing, you could let him listen to this recording of the voice that you say you have."

Lo Curto began to hedge on this one, murmuring that it was against the law to record a phone conversation without the other party's knowledge. I suspected that he'd never recorded the conversation in the first place.

It was hard talking to him. He wouldn't make any admissions or promises. Just a big smoke screen of double-talk and legal phrases. He was too cagey, too masterful for me. I felt like a fat man.

He hadn't told me a damn thing in return for my information. It was frustrating. My face must have mirrored my thoughts for I suddenly found him smiling at me, as if he felt sorry for me.

"What are *your* plans?" he asked.

"I want to clear up this mess. I want you to drop the charges against me and Gilbert. Then, back to business as usual."

Smiling some more, he toyed with his coffee cup and asked how I'd gotten mixed up in the affair.

"It's a long story."

The lawyer was suppressing a laugh. I felt foolish.

"You should never have become involved," he said. "It's not too late to get out, you know."

I nodded, not quite sure what he meant. Then I finished my coffee and, trying to put a little briskness into my voice, asked what I should tell Gilbert that night.

It was no use. Lo Curto still wouldn't give me a straight answer. He just snowed me with his legal jargon. Like big, flabby, formless snowflakes the words came down . . . whereas and to wit . . . beyond a reasonable doubt . . . responsibility of a third party . . . party of the first part . . .

14

Gilbert had invited me to his apartment for dinner that night. His wife and kids were going to Washington for the weekend.

I took the subway to a station about five blocks from his address. As I walked along I could see another one of those big white apartment houses in the distance.

There was a crowd up ahead. Police cars, their red lights flashing, were double-parked. I quickened my steps, then I slowed up. Somehow I had the feeling that it was bad news.

Now I was closer to the white bulk that loomed up into the night air. There was a funny sensation in the pit of my stomach. My shoe leather slapped helplessly against the pavement. More people were gathering. The cops were keeping them back from a white sheet that covered something just to the left of the flashy entrance.

I showed a cop my I.D. card and he let me through.

"Who is it?"

"Guy named Gilbert."

The pang of certainty made me sick. Several other detectives moved my way. A voice asked if I knew anything about it.

"I was coming to see him. What happened?"

"Looks like he came from his own apartment. See that open window up there—the one near the air conditioner? If he'd a jumped from the roof he'd a been really squashed."

"What do you mean—jumped?"

"Jumped or fell."

They said I could look at the body. When I lifted the sheet part way, some people in the crowd gasped theatrically like they're supposed to do. I guess it was Gilbert, all right. The same curly iron-gray hair. But the face and skull were badly smashed; it's always a shock to see how soft the brain really is. One hand was attached only by skin, and blood was soaking through his shirt.

I dropped the sheet.

"You say it wasn't suicide?" a detective asked.

"It was murder."

"What makes you so sure?"

"I knew him. He was in no mood to commit suicide. He was cooking dinner for me tonight. But even if I didn't know him, this doesn't look like suicide and you know it."

They crowded around me again, their faces unfriendly. No one likes an outsider who comes in and shoots off his mouth. One of them, a guy with a ruddy face like Flannery, said:

"Keep talkin', mac."

"Well, look at the position of the body. How far out from the building is it—twelve feet, fifteen feet?"

Turning as one, they measured the distance with their eyes. "So what?" the red-faced one said. "He could have launched himself. He could have crouched on the window-sill and leaped out."

"Horsefeathers!"

"All right," the spokesman said. "Why couldn't he?"

"He's still wearing his shoes. If he was going to balance himself like you say, he'd have taken his shoes off. Besides, if he was going to launch himself, he'd have used his terrace. Isn't that his terrace up there?"

They were silent, their grim faces grudgingly conceding the truth of what I'd said. But I had additional points to make. For example, the fourth floor wasn't so high: most jumpers would have gone from the roof to make sure.

96

What's more, nine out of ten jumpers were considerate enough to go from the rear of a building. Invariably the body is found in a rear courtyard.

The detectives were silent. They knew all these things as well as I did.

"I bet there wasn't a suicide note," I added.

"I don't know, we just got here. Let's go up to the apartment now. You come along, Sherlock."

The doorman had deserted his post so the front door stopped us momentarily. This was no problem for the detectives. They got in by pressing all the buttons on the bellboard. As we zoomed upward in a big elevator, I pointed out that Gilbert had access to guns, drugs, and other things. He could have killed himself more neatly than this.

"Don't oversell," a detective grunted.

The super came along and let us into apartment 4C, which was furnished something like the funeral home. A heavy odor of spices drew us to the kitchen and its simmering pots and pans. Red spaghetti sauce. Sausages, sweet and hot. Pale-green artichokes, their spiky leaves beginning to spread, and some unidentified frying objects.

Next, the living room with its red carpet and lush armchairs. A white piano. A massive TV console. Bottles of liquor and various tidbits on a small table. Cocktail napkins marked "His" and "Hearse."

We didn't find the usual two suicide notes—the one about love and the one about the money.

But to tell the truth, we didn't find any signs of a life-and-death struggle, either. A few magazines had fallen off a table, but that was all. Then a detective and I examined the windowsill. No scrapes, no scuffs, as might have been made by Gilbert's shoes if he had launched himself from here.

"Don't touch anything," the red-faced detective said. "We'll dust for prints."

I think it was the aroma of the Italian dinner that

convinced them it wasn't suicide because a jumper doesn't worry about food. On the other hand, they weren't sold yet that it was murder. It could be an accident. "Death under suspicious circumstances pending further investigation" would be the immediate verdict.

But I knew different.

I had to answer a lot of questions. The cops already knew about the exhumation, the missing body, Gilbert's arrest, and so on. It's their job to know these things.

"You say it was murder," one of them said to me. "So who killed him?"

"I don't know."

"You got any theories?"

"Yes. He was looking for the man who stole the coffin. Maybe that man thought he was getting too close."

"Was he getting close?"

"He might have been."

I didn't want to tell them about Hendriques' confession or the phone call offering to return the body.

Cops aren't so bad. This talk about police brutality is mostly bunk. Cops do chisel a lot, but it's mainly petty stuff like having their wedding pictures taken free by the Detective Photo Unit.

They let me look through the contents of Gilbert's wallet before I left. His birthday turned out to be June 17 and this figured. You see, men of Gilbert's age are most likely to kill themselves on their birthdays and he hadn't. Just another little point that argued against suicide. I didn't mention it aloud, though. I didn't want to oversell.

On the walk back to the subway I called Lo Curto from a phone booth. I wanted to know if he'd had any more phone calls about the body.

"No," he said.

"Did you tell anyone what I told you this afternoon— that Gilbert had found out about DiMaio's part in this?"

"No." A pause. "I didn't even tell my nephews."

98

"I see."

"Why do you ask?"

"Gilbert's dead. It looks like he was murdered."

"But that's impossible, unbelievable! What happened?"

He wanted to cross-examine me but I wasn't in the mood for it. I said I'd talk to him later.

The subway train was crowded. It rattled along the dusty tunnel. I kept my head down because I didn't want to look at the other passengers just then.

After a while the train stopped at a station. Shoes were moving over dirty squares of gray and blue tile. Seconds later I heard the doors close and the train was off, rattling and rumbling, gaining speed, leaving Gilbert farther and farther behind.

He was far away now, somewhere back there down the dark corridors of the tunnel, lost and gone, and I was going on without him. I had to leave him back there because he was dead.

Gilbert. My friend.

The train began slowing down. Another station. Shoes moving on a dirty floor. All kinds of shoes. Black shoes and brown. Square-toed workmen's shoes. Pointed shoes to catch the cockroaches in the corners . . .

I looked up. Limp faces were swaying like dishcloths on a line. They didn't know me or Gilbert, and they didn't want to know us. They didn't give a damn. Eight million faces, and nobody gave a damn.

Except one.

The murderer.

Somehow he'd learned that Hendriques had talked, that we were making progress, maybe closing in. So he'd killed Gilbert. And I might be next on the list.

It was so ridiculous I could almost laugh. From the first I'd never wanted any part of the stolen body. Hadn't I told everybody to count me out? Yet here I was, in deeper than ever, plodding along in reel 3.

Because that's where we were in the script. The part where the hero's buddy is murdered and he's supposed to swear vengeance. It was crazy. Why wasn't somebody yelling "Cut"?

The train was slowing up. A sign said *CONCOURSE SQUARE*. I got out and walked quickly up the stairs.

A blast of cold air hit me as I reached the street. Bundling up my overcoat, I started for home. Wait a minute.

I turned around and watched the exit. I wanted to be sure I hadn't been followed. But no one else came up the stairs. I turned once more toward home, wondering if my imagination was getting the better of me.

Five blocks isn't really so long in the daytime or in the summer. But if you've ever walked five city blocks in winter, late at night when there's nobody around—or so it seems—you know it's a different proposition. The pavement stretches far away into the darkness and, even though you hurry, each block seems longer and more lonely. The time stretches also, winding out forever like a great watch spring, and you're alert and ready, glancing right and left, wondering if there's someone concealed behind that bush or in that doorway.

Sure, the social workers say that the people lurking in the shadows just want money for food—or maybe for drugs. But let's be fair. There's another school of thought.

The criminologists say that in many cases robbery is only an excuse, a cover-up. The shadow people want to kill. And the killing is a cover-up for something deeper. The killing is a sex crime.

I usually don't worry about muggers. But tonight I had a reason to be jumpy. I'd just seen Gilbert with his head smashed in.

At the first corner I crossed against the red light, my shoes scuffing and scuffling over some broken pavement as I reached the curb. A streetlamp stood there, a lonely torch burning in silence. Beyond it, the street was darker.

100

It was just a narrow one-way street, a black corridor converging to a vanishing point, here and there made grayish by the light from other streetlamps. It wasn't totally silent; from time to time a car droned in the distance and there was a scrap of youthful laughter. But all these sounds were far away. The only real live sound was that of my footsteps rapping on the pavement.

I glanced over my shoulder. There was no one there.

Quickly I passed the houses, their blank faces pitted with dead windows. Another corner. Another streetlight. I crossed at the intersection. Another block. I passed the dead windows as my footsteps echoed behind me.

Those weren't echoes—

There was a guy behind me, about half a block away, coming fast. He was losing no time. His hat was pulled down, his chin wrapped in a dark muffler or something. I couldn't even see his eyes. The rapid tapping of his feet more than matched mine. He was closing the gap between us.

I speeded up. Not that I was really afraid. He was probably just a guy who'd left a house after a party or a shackup. But even as my heels beat double-time against the pavement, the staccato sounds behind me quickened. A backward glance told me that he was closer now, striding like the wind.

A corner, a red light—an excuse for me to run across, my coat collar flapping in the cold air. I gained a lap on him by this maneuver and for a moment the sounds in back of me faded to a soft patter. Then they came back, faster and louder, as he too ran across the intersection.

I looked back. The traffic light was a great green eye.

I didn't want to run but I was doing the next thing to it, really covering ground now, racking up the mileage. My feet pounded past rows and rows of vacant windows as the streetlamps marked the way. He was still behind me but he wasn't gaining any more.

Two more blocks. I hadn't walked this fast in years.

There was a stitch in my side, quite painful, but I kept moving. Tick-tack noises echoed after me, now fainter, now almost a block behind. It was pretty obvious that this guy wasn't trying to catch me. Just the same, I kept going.

The final block. I looked back once more. Across the rim of the night sky I saw the silhouettes of the big buildings on Concourse Square—the YMCA, the hospital, the courthouse, the funeral home. They had Gilbert now. They stood there—waiting.

15

No sooner was I home than the phone rang. It was Andy with a message that Mr. Primavera wanted to see me.

"Now?"

"Yeah, I can drive you up in no time."

"I know."

It was eleven o'clock by my watch. I said okay. But when Mother found out I was leaving she grumbled:

"When are you going to stop this nonsense?"

"It shouldn't be much longer, Mom."

"I won't be here much longer."

Andy was outside in the souped-up green sedan. We had the road to ourselves. He talked a lot, telling me what a great guy Gilbert had been, and I was inclined to agree. Yes, Gilbert had tried to use me, but it hadn't been a one-way street.

We swept along the parkway. This was the third time in little over a month that I'd been on the upstate road. I hoped it would be the last. I watched for the place where the Hertz car had gone over—a shiny new guard rail marked the spot. Soon we turned off the parkway and the sedan rode softly over the country road. Stripped trees waved to us. I heard the crunch of gravel as the headlights picked up the blurred outline of the mansion in the distance. As we approached, a shaggy creature moved across the lawn on all fours. It was too big to be a man.

"Did he get an Irish wolfhound?" I asked.

"Yeah. Biggest goddamn thing I ever saw."

Mr. Primavera opened the door himself. His face was very sad, the mystified wrinkled face of an old monkey. He showed me into the library and said:

"This is a terrible thing. His wife and children don't know yet."

"Yes."

"It's terrible what's been happening. It seems that one of our own men started all this, and now it's just one crime after another."

I nodded.

"What's happening to the world? All this murder and crime and lawlessness—life isn't worth living when people act this way . . . Oh, sit down, Mr. Talbot."

When I was comfortable he asked what I thought.

I shrugged. "It's only theory."

"Tell me anyway."

Step by step I went through the whole megillah with him, reviewing the sequence of events, the confession of Dr. Hendriques, the assertions of James Lo Curto. I pointed out the crucial fact that everything had been quiet until DiMaio was officially declared dead. It was my theory that the man who had taken the body had become afraid that Gilbert was closing in on him.

"But why should he think that?" Mr. Primavera asked.

"Because the doctor confessed. Somehow, DiMaio's accomplice found out that the doctor had talked."

"He would have to find out from somebody," the old man said.

"That's right. Now, the only person I told was James Lo Curto and he says he didn't tell anyone else. That leaves the doctor and Gilbert himself—"

"Mr. Talbot."

"Yes?"

"Excuse me for interrupting you. I can't follow what you are saying. My old mind can't keep up . . . but it is not

104

important that I understand. I want you to find out who killed Gilbert. I don't care about the coffin or anything else now. Just find out who killed Gilbert."

"I'd like to, but there isn't much to go on. I don't have any leads to follow, not any good ones, anyway. The man who killed Gilbert may be right under my nose—he may even think that I'm close on his trail—but it's not so."

"You mean you think it's someone from the funeral home?"

"It's quite possible. It would have to be someone in the funeral business. Otherwise he wouldn't have been able to get the coffin at the airport so easily, and he wouldn't know how to handle it."

"You'll check the people at the funeral home?"

"Yes."

"But there are many people working there. You don't know all of them."

"I know. That makes it harder."

"I'll give you an army," Mr. Primavera said quietly. "Guns, men, cars, money, anything you need."

It was the best offer I'd had all day. Besides, I'd never had an army before. I was tempted to take him up on it as some of my childhood fantasies came back to me. Big Clem Talbot, sitting in the back of a long gray ghost car. Behind the wheel, my bodyguard, a terrifying mug with no forehead.

"I mean this, Mr. Talbot."

"I know you do, but I think I'd work better alone. I'll call you if I need anything."

"Can't you use some help now?"

"No, not really. It's not a question of muscle. Somebody has to think this thing through."

"Won't you need money?"

"No. Just brains, Mr. Primavera."

"Ah, that is more difficult to supply." He was smiling a sad little smile.

A noise outside caused me to look through the library

doors. It was only Andy mixing himself a drink. I wondered if he'd been listening. Could he be DiMaio's accomplice? It was possible. Skinny though he was, he somehow looked strong enough to handle a coffin. And he certainly would know his way around the airport.

But one thing didn't fit: at the airport the thief had banged his car into the warehouse door, something an ace driver would never do.

There wasn't much more to talk about. Andy brought me a drink. I jotted down Mr. Primavera's phone number and he said:

"Call me at any time. A man my age doesn't sleep."

Another five minutes found him standing at the front door, ignoring the raw gusts of wind, as Andy started the sedan. "God bless you," he called, waving his hand like Judge Hardy would do in those old pictures Mother watches on TV.

It may seem odd to compare a leader of the Syndicate with Judge Hardy, yet it really isn't. It so happens that the mob has a heart. They wouldn't keep a man in a coal mine his whole life. They even have their own Social Security System. Every Friday night at a place near one of the bridges that lead out of Manhattan, old and disabled men come, former workers for the mob now down on their luck, and each one gets his little envelope. It's part of what the Italians call *cambiale*.

Besides, Mr. Primavera was a great family man. His ideas may have been old-fashioned according to modern standards, but in his own way he tried to protect his children. Gilbert had once told me about the old man's interview with his prospective son-in-law.

"You wanna marry with my daughter?"

"Yes sir."

"All right. I give you my blessing, but there's a just one thing—"

"Yes, sir?"

"There's no divorce in this family—you understand?"

"Yes."

"You coulda die, but you coulda not get a divorce—you understand?"

"(*Gulp*) Yes, sir."

16

After a few hours' sleep I woke up to face a gray December day. I felt low and depressed and at first I couldn't figure out why. Then I remembered. Gilbert was dead.

It was the day after the murder. Mr. Primavera had asked me to find the killer, and both of us were inclined to think that it was someone from the funeral home. But this didn't mean that the search had been narrowed down—quite the opposite.

Funeral homes employ an awful lot of people. In addition to the front men who procure the bodies, the embalmers and cosmeticians who prepare them, and the hearse drivers who take them away, a million little jobs have to be done.

Someone has to run to the Board of Health with the death certificates, phone obituary notices to the newspapers, get American flags from the V.A. Someone has to deal with the florists, the casket makers, the printers, and the clergy. Supplies must be ordered and stocked; so many cases of embalming fluid, so many yards of mummy wrapping, so many coffins, cheap or expensive, metal or wood, regular or extra large. A funeral home is open seven days a week and, when they say they'll bury you, they have to mean it.

The Jewish funeral homes even have additional personnel. One is the *shamus*, the man who watches the body. This word has been used to mean detective, but a real *shamus* is nothing like that. He's a little old man who reads a Hebrew prayerbook—and that means he reads from right to left.

There is also the *schlepper,* lowest of the low, he-who-drags-out-the-body. When someone dies, the *schleppers* have to go after him, even if he's some two-hundred-pounder on the fifth floor of a walk-up. They have to put this body, often as not decomposed, into a musty green canvas body bag and carry it down the stairs in the middle of the night. They break their hump.

Unless no one is watching—

In which case the *schleppers* make it easy on themselves by using a rapid transit system. A series of kicks sends the body down the steps, crashing into the wall at every turn, things that go bump in the night. It's in critical condition when it arrives at the funeral home. A call goes out:

Code three.

Emergency.

Calling Clive Andresen.

Anyway, the point I'm making is that there were a lot of possible suspects at the funeral home. For all I knew, DiMaio might have recruited some florist or *schlepper* or hearse driver whom I'd never seen.

Faced with the job of interviewing all these people, no wonder I decided to concentrate on things.

Unfortunately, the physical clues in the case were few. I ticked them off on my fingers. There was the red wig, the paint from the station wagon and the signature on the bill of lading. In addition, James Lo Curto claimed to have a tape recording of the voice of a man trying to sell back the stolen body.

I decided to check on the wig first.

All I knew about the wig business was that it had taken an upswing during World War II because of the scalpings. The person indirectly responsible was a blond actress named

Veronica Lake. About 1940 she appeared in some Hollywood films wearing a unique hair-do in which a bang covered one eye and half her face. Lots of young girls copied her, just about the same time that they went into the war factories, and you can guess the rest. One minute you'd have a pretty girl in front of a whirring machine . . .

After breakfast I consulted the telephone directory over a second cup of coffee. Hair goods, I found out, is the general name for the trade in wigs, wiglets, chignons, clusters, falls, braids, ponytails, hairpieces, toupees, layaways, problem pieces, and transformations. Who would have guessed it was so complicated?

There were more than a hundred places dealing in the stuff, but luckily most of them didn't cater to men. I narrowed my list down to twenty-one places and, since it was Saturday, they were bound to be open.

The first one I hit was Hair Haven, Inc., a big fancy salon on one of the better avenues in Manhattan. A sign in the window stated that there were separate departments for men and women, private booths on request, and also private home consultations.

Picking my way through a bedlam of shrill overdressed women, I came to the Men's Department. It was lined with rows and rows of glass cases containing dummy heads with hairpieces of all colors and styles draped over them. A guy with wavy black hair and a thin mustache waltzed toward me.

"Was that a cleaning or a restyling?"

"Come again."

"What can we do for you?" His eyes were on my hair. "That's authentic human hair, isn't it?"

"Yes."

"It's a beautiful job."

"Thank you."

"What did you want done?" he persisted.

When I showed him my identification, his manner became distant. I must realize, he said, that his clients were very sensitive. Besides, some were V.I.P.s whose privacy must be respected.

"No one will know I talked to you," I told him.

"I'm sorry, but I can't cooperate in this."

"Would you rather talk to the police?"

"If this were a police matter, they would have been here already."

"Not necessarily. A crime was committed and the perpetrator wore a red wig. If you won't talk to me, I'll find some ambitious cop who'll talk to you."

"Are you threatening me?"

"Of course I'm threatening you."

That slowed him. I gave him a minute to think it over. Behind him a sign on a wall said *LOOK YOUNGER, LOOK TALLER*. Finally he said:

"All right. What do you want to know?"

"I'd like you to check your records for a three-month period, beginning about last August. I want to know if you outfitted anyone with a red wig during that time."

"We don't get many calls for red wigs."

"That should make it easy."

Going to a small desk he picked up a notebook and flipped through it. "What tone—I mean, what shade—of red?"

"I don't know. Any shade."

"There's a wide spectrum of reds, you know. Auburn and strawberry blond, all the way down the line to carrot-top."

"I see."

He had only two names for me. Hyman Gelbstein, 2366 East Fourteenth Street, had been outfitted with an auburn toupee, authentic human hair, on September third. And Porfirio Karezza, 717 Abingdon Square, had had his synthetic auburn toupee restyled for the mod look on October 20. Well, I'd look these two guys up and, if either of them had any connection with the funeral business, the hairs of his head would really be numbered.

I thanked the guy and turned to leave, but he called me back. "May I say something?"

"Sure."

"A red wig for a man is very unusual. I don't think a man who wanted to keep his identity secret would get a red wig."

"This one did."

"I'm sorry—I didn't express myself clearly. I mean he might get a red wig, but it wouldn't be a man's toupee. Do you follow me?"

"You mean he'd get a woman's wig?"

"Yes. It would be easier just to buy a woman's wig and trim it down."

"You're sure this could be done?"

"Oh, certainly."

The guy had a point there. The way he'd suggested was the better way—faster, safer, and more convenient. No doubt about it. And this meant, of course, that my present efforts were a waste of time. I listened as he spoke again:

"But why would a criminal get a *red* wig? Isn't a disguise supposed to make you *less* conspicuous?"

"I've already asked myself that question," I said. "I don't know the answer."

I was glad to get out of there. Even the small chance of tracing the thief through the wig had been taken from me. Outside it was raining, and the rain fitted my mood. I threw away my list of addresses as the rain beat down on my authentic human hair. Instead of another salon, I settled for a saloon.

The alcohol seemed to make me think more clearly. I got musing about the early beginnings of the case, my dates with Mrs. DiMaio, the places I'd been with her, her good looks and her auburn hair—

It was a hunch I had to follow.

At our last phone conversation she'd blamed me for the death of her husband. Scum of the earth, she'd called me, murderer, sneaking coward, and a few other things. Still, I had to try her again. I went to the pay phone in the back of the saloon.

"What do *you* want?"

She wasn't hysterical now. I said maybe we could exchange some information.

"I have nothing to say to you, now or anytime."

"Mrs. DiMaio, don't hang up. Listen. Your husband was killed accidentally. Someday I'll tell you about it. But a man from the funeral home was murdered yesterday . . ."

"Who?"

"Gilbert."

"Oh. I didn't know. He phoned me yesterday . . ."

"Did Gilbert tell you that this doctor confessed?"

A long pause. "Yes."

"And that he implicated your husband?"

"Yes."

"Have you told anyone what Gilbert told you?"

"Wait. I can't think. This is such a shock. I can't remember telling anyone . . ."

For the next few minutes I was busy answering her questions about her husband's role in the theft of the coffin. I told everything I knew in the hope she'd reciprocate. Finally I asked:

"Would you answer some questions for me?"

"Such as?"

It was at this moment that a drunk tried to get me out of the phone booth. I knew he had no one to phone, but this is what drunks pull when they're in the pugnacious stage. The door of the booth rattled as a thick voice bellowed that I'd been in there twenty minutes. Opening the door, I shoved a dollar at him and said my wife was having a baby.

He went away.

"Hello?" I said into the phone.

"I'm still here."

"I wanted to ask if you had a red wig that was stolen?"

"That's a ridiculous question. Are you drunk or something?"

Eventually she told me that she had a reddish wig that was missing. She'd missed it lately, thought it might have been thrown out accidentally. But why was I asking?

"The man who stole the coffin was wearing a red wig."

"You think it was mine?"

"Yes. Is it possible that the wig could have disappeared before you separated from your husband?"

"Yes, I suppose it is. I wouldn't have been wearing it during the summer . . ."

Her answers to my other questions were not as helpful. She insisted that DiMaio had no real estate—at least, the lawyers for the estate hadn't found any—and no close friends.

"Could he have a friend from a different funeral home?"

"No, not that I know of."

The drunk was back now, so I thanked Mrs. DiMaio and went out into the rain. Fortunately, it was letting up. I walked along, thinking over the afternoon's work. Another little piece had been fitted into the puzzle, a small detail that in itself was nothing, and yet everything.

It was helping me to fill in the picture. A picture of a crime that was very local, very parochial, very close to home. DiMaio didn't seem to have strayed any distance at all from his own back yard. He'd used only the people and the materials close at hand.

Me for the alibi, Hendriques for the outlet, and his wife's red wig for the disguise. It was a self-contained, local operation, almost a family affair, and it suggested one more thing:

To be consistent, he would have planned to hide the coffin somewhere close by. And if so, then the man who'd actually taken it might be close by also, watching over it, wondering how he could dispose of it, guarding it jealously.

Just a second.

The coffin might be very near. Maybe I passed it daily without knowing how close I was—

But a coffin is real, tangible, it's big and it can be found. And it figured that if I could find the coffin, I'd probably find the killer.

17

Somewhat later that same evening I found myself at the Rump and Romp working on the blue-plate special. The peas could have been Civil War surplus musket balls. At a nearby table I saw the horny profile of Clive Andresen.

"That was a rum thing that happened in Kenya. Too bad about old Abercrombie. You remember him. Stiff graying mustache. Military strut."

"Yes, whatever happened to old Abercrombie?"

"Ran off into the bush, don't you know. Ran off to live with some bloody chimpanzee."

"Was it a female chimpanzee?"

"Of course, man! Nothing queer about old Abercrombie."

All I'm saying is that Andresen had the face to go with the story. He didn't even need a pith helmet. His golden amber eyes were following Helen about the room. Those old eyes must have looked on a lot of evil. He must have had a lot of experience in his eerie profession. Maybe he was the guy I should be talking to.

This idea gathered force as I choked on the powdery almond cake and sipped my coffee. He was still at his table, watching Helen, catching her eye whenever he could, smiling at her with his bristly military mustache.

I asked her to sound him out. All she had to say was that she had a friend who wanted to consult him on a technical matter.

His face brightened when she went to speak to him, and he nodded several times. She looked doubtful. I saw him glance my way and stop smiling. Then they talked some more before she came back to my table.

"He says all right, but he won't talk here. He wants both of us to come to his house."

"That's all right with me." But when I realized that she didn't look too happy about the idea, I added: "If you wouldn't mind going. It means a lot to me."

"Okay. I get off at nine. I'll tell him we'll be over as soon as we can."

"Thanks, Helen—"

But she was already walking back to his table. About ten minutes later he left, looking rather pleased with himself. His eyes met mine for the barest second.

Helen wasn't talking much in the taxi. "Listen," I said, "I have the feeling that you're not anxious to go."

"Well, to tell the truth, I'm not and it's not because I don't like him. He's all right at the restaurant. It's just that he's too—eager."

"We'll try not to stay long."

The taxi dropped us off in front of a fairly big house in a good neighborhood. It was set back from the street, and you reached it by a slate path that snaked its way through beds of dead flowers. I heard music from a piano but it sounded odd; there was no bounce to it and yet it wasn't spidery like classical music.

"Listen," Helen said.

"I hear it."

The music got louder, but not better, as we came to the front door. It sounded thin and cold like icicles, like something Woodrow Wilson might play: I could hardly associate it with Andresen. However, when we rang the bell the music stopped and it was he who showed us into a big room with red and brown leather chairs, a piano and a small bar. His hands caressed Helen's shoulders as he took off her coat, and I looked the other way.

"Was that you playing?" she asked him.

"Yes. The truth now—how did you like it?"

"Well, it was different."

"What did it sound like to you?" He guided her to a chair.

"Very serious. Like church music."

"Very good. You're absolutely right." He held up two twisted hands. "You see, with my arthritis I can't play octaves any more. I have to harmonize with what they call the fourths and fifths and that's the music of the Middle Ages."

A moment of silence. Everyone was looking at his twisted hands. He moved the fingers awkwardly.

"Can't you take something for it?" Helen asked.

"Ah, but I do, I do. I take cortisone. Unfortunately, cortisone has certain side effects which I'll leave to your imagination."

Oh, no, I thought.

"What will you have to drink?"

The Scotch he poured was the same color as his amber eyes. Golden flecks of light seemed to bounce back and forth between his highball glass and his eyes. I felt sorry that he was so hyped up.

We got to my problem about ten minutes later. But when I explained that I was on the trail of a stolen body, he all but laughed in my face. "What would I know about stolen bodies?"

"Nothing. But you've been in the undertaking business and you might know your way around—"

"There are hundreds of undertakers in this city," he said, toying with his glass. "Why come to me?"

"I just heard you were more successful than most—er, more resourceful—"

118

"Resourceful," he said. "I like that word. I'll have to write it down." He looked straight at me. "Are you calling me a crook?"

"No. You're putting words in my mouth."

"Then what do you mean by calling me resourceful?"

"I heard you were a troubleshooter. I heard you could help people who were in a jam."

"Are you in trouble?"

"In a way."

"What do you want to know?"

I leaned forward. "If you had a body, how would you get rid of it?"

Helen gasped, I heard her. Her lips were partly open. Andresen's glance was momentarily directed at her, then back to me, and he asked:

"Do you go out with women often?"

"No, but that's neither here nor there. I came here for some information on a technical problem. I'm sorry if I put the question so bluntly."

He turned back to Helen and asked if the discussion was disturbing her. She said no. He was suave and solicitous, and he was beginning to get me mad.

"In that case," he said, "I'll answer your question by saying that I'd embalm the body and get rid of it a piece at a time."

"I guess I put my question badly. Suppose you had to hide a body in this city. Suppose the body was in a coffin in a station wagon. Suppose it was one o'clock in the afternoon and you had to be back on your job by two. Where would you hide this coffin?"

"In a funeral home."

"Suppose that was impossible."

"Let me think a minute." He took another swallow of Scotch. I couldn't read Helen's expression.

"It would have to be someplace in the city," I prompted.

"Yes, yes."

After thinking a minute or so, he said he'd hide it in a cemetery.

"You'd bury it?"

"No. But I could hide it very quickly in a cemetery. Remember that I'm resourceful."

"How could I forget it?"

My remark must have struck him as sarcastic and so, I guess to punish me, he let me hang a little longer. I leaned back in my chair and took a big drink of Scotch. At last he said:

"In a mausoleum."

"Ahhhhhh." The noise came from deep in my throat.

I was wrapped up in my own thoughts for the next few minutes, only dimly aware that he'd poured more drinks and was leaning over Helen's chair, whispering things to her. Somewhere very far away I heard her laugh. But I wasn't in the room any more; I was in the station wagon as the man with the red wig and the dark glasses maneuvered it through the early afternoon traffic. We were going down the Van Wyck Expressway at a steady thirty-five, keeping in the extreme right-hand lane. An accident now would ruin the plan.

I'm in the back of the wagon with the coffin. It's covered by a tarpaulin. It doesn't slide or bounce because the man behind the wheel is being very careful. The airport attendant said he was a lousy driver, yet so far he's doing all right. But he's silent and I haven't seen his face. Just his big hands on the wheel.

Now they shift position.

The wagon turns off the expressway and stops for a red light. Then it moves on again, cruising slowly.

A funeral home on the right. We pass it. Several more blocks go by. Cars. Trucks. Pedestrians. We're in the middle of the city with a stolen coffin, but no one gives us a second glance. DiMaio's plan is working.

Another few blocks, a different section of the city. The wagon is still moving cautiously. We pass a church and another funeral home. A big clock says it's after one. And still he hasn't said a word, the faceless man behind the wheel. He doesn't know I'm there. More blocks go by, more traffic lights. It can't be much longer.

The wagon slows.

Up ahead I see a cemetery, the trees, the tombstones, the iron gates. And now the wagon is signaling for a right turn.

No one stops us. We're going down the service road. Graves are everywhere. I don't see many people because it's after one and the funerals are over. Here and there red and yellow flower wreaths lie on the hard winter earth or the harder stone. We're moving down a road lined by a high hedge, and here we make a turn. Now we're coming to the end of the service road, the outskirts of the burial grounds, quiet, deserted. Even the traffic noises are muffled. There's no one here but the dead and they won't tell.

The wagon stops.

Yes, Clive Andresen was right. A square stone building stands here, a family mausoleum. I can't read the name chiseled in the stone above the door. But the driver knows, and already he's at the back of the station wagon and the tailgate is coming down.

A low stretcher with four rubber wheels, light and noiseless. He takes it out and sets it on the ground. Now he's reaching for the coffin. He drags it out on top of the stretcher—drags it out easily, for he's a big man. He turns toward the mausoleum. Too bad I can't read that name above the door.

A minute. Two minutes.

Then he's back with the stretcher and once more we're on our way. Behind us the mausoleum seems unchanged, just like before. But with us it's different because he's speeding through the traffic as if he doesn't give a damn. There's no red wig any more, no dark glasses—and yet I still can't see his face.

It doesn't matter for the moment.

The important thing is that he pulled it off. He hid the body in a place selected by DiMaio. And that means—if we're going by the M.O.—that it's not the mausoleum of a stranger . . .

18

"No, that's all for me," Helen said.

I came out of my reverie as Andresen was trying to freshen up her drink. Her glass was still half full. He was holding her arm playfully with one of his arthritic hands.

"No, really, that's enough."

My second drink was untouched. I downed it quickly and asked for a refill, forcing him to give her a breathing spell. I knew he was giving her a hard time, but I did feel indebted to him. He'd come through for me as I'd hoped, showing me how simple it would have been to conceal the coffin. After all, how often do people go to inspect their mausoleums?

What's more, he'd even given me the hope of possibly finding this particular mausoleum. Not that this gave him the right to bother Helen—

He was after her again.

I moved my chair over near them and tried to create a diversion. Even so, it was about fifteen minutes more before we got out of there. Once again, Andresen made a big production about Helen's coat, keeping his arm around her above and beyond the call of duty.

As we picked our way down the garden path, poorly illuminated as it was, the piano struck up once more and the hollow sounds seemed to hang in the air, old and incomplete.

"I'm sorry if he bothered you." I said.

"It's all right."

"He really helped me, I think."

"That's all that counts."

"So you are mad. I'm sorry, Helen, but what was I to do? You could handle him, couldn't you?"

She didn't answer right away. But as we walked on farther, she said quietly:

"You think I'm used to this stuff because I'm a waitress, don't you?"

"I didn't say that."

"You didn't have to. Well, I'll tell you something: you're right. I'm used to it and I wouldn't need any help from you to fracture his skull. But I didn't want to fracture his skull. He's not a bad guy. I have a certain respect for him."

"Then what are you so mad about?"

"You. All you care about is getting what you want."

I put my arm about her. "Listen—"

She shook my arm off.

"I'm sorry," I said. "Tonight was very important for me. It was part of my job."

"Why can't you get a decent job? Why do you have to be mixed up in all this horrible stuff?"

"Every case isn't like this."

"I should hope not."

We didn't talk much more. When I got her home I noticed that her eyes looked red. I apologized some more. This time I think she believed me.

Just the same I felt like a crumb, leaving. Any resemblance between me and a man was purely coincidental.

From the nearest candy store I phoned the funeral home. When Gino answered I asked when the funeral would be.

"Monday, it looks like. The body is still in the morgue. They didn't do the autopsy yet."

"Will they do it tomorrow?"

"Yeah. The head doc promised. We oughta be able to pick the body up tomorrow sometime."

"Is the family back yet?"

"Yeah. They're all broken up."

"How about his father and mother?"

"They're both dead."

"Just as well. Where is he being buried?"

"St. Charles'."

"Does he have a family plot?"

"Naw. They got one of them mausoleums."

19

At midnight I was on my way to see Werner at the Montefiore Zionist Chapel. I needed some more technical information.

Werner's real name is John O'Mara. He uses the name Werner for professional reasons. Although I'd known him for many years, I'd never really gotten used to the sight of him wearing the yarmulka, or skullcap. Somehow, when you see a black skullcap, you expect to find a thin tortured face under it, and maybe a long white beard. But Werner's face is nothing like that. It's sort of obscene, the sight of all those freckles under a yarmulka.

For another thing, he has keyhole eyes. They're so close together he can look through a keyhole with both eyes at the same time.

This funeral home is Orthodox, but there are several Orthodox groups. The most conservative one insists on the mikvah, the ceremonial washing of the body with water. The water must be caught in cisterns and flow through natural passageways in rock on its way to the tub. It's a biblical thing, something about water and rock. After the mikvah, the water may be drained off through brass plumbing.

None of the Orthodox groups go in for embalming—they even bore holes in the bottom of the coffin to let the worms in. Werner keeps the bodies overnight in special coffins in the cellar. These coffins are lined with zinc and the bodies, wrapped in white sheets, are covered with ice cubes for refrigeration. There's also a small, round glass window in the cover of each coffin to permit viewing of the body. I remember Werner once saying that Lincoln was in a coffin like this.

"Hello," Werner said. "Long time, no see."

He didn't look much older. His face was a little redder than I remembered. There was a drink on his desk.

Mother never did like him.

"Sit down. Let me pour you a drink."

"Thanks."

"You want ice?"

"No, never mind."

"Hey," Werner said, "before I forget—are you coming with us to the Morgue Man's Ball?"

"I'm not sure."

"They're having Marty Nussbaum's band."

"I'll let you know."

"Come with us. You haven't had a day off since Pearl Harbor."

Every winter the United Mortuary Workers from Local 420, AFL-CIO, hold a dinner dance at a big restaurant on Long Island. It's known as the Morgue Man's Ball. Undertakers, homicide detectives, doctors, and others in the death industries go to it. I hadn't been there since I broke up with the girl from American Express.

She'd been too bossy, anyway. "If you call for me just once more wearing one of those blue serge suits from the nineteen-forties, I won't go out with you . . ."

"I'll let you know," I told Werner again.

"What's with you? You look worried. You ought to change your brand of embalming fluid."

Despite all his talk and jokes, it seemed to me that he was jumpy. He downed his drink and immediately poured another big one. I asked what was the matter.

"Oh, I had an accident today."

"With your car?"

"No. I was screwing around down in the preparation room near this body. It was from a hospital, all wrapped up in that white paper they use to save money—looked like a goddamned Christmas present. So, anyhow, I'm standing near this guy for about half an hour before I take the wrappings off and, when I do, I see these red marks painted on his face and I know what that means."

"What?"

"Radiation therapy, for Christ's sake! I look closer and find a tag on him saying that this body must be handled with precautions because it contains radioactive material. But this tag is under the paper he's wrapped in! Some schmuck wrapped him this way—can you imagine? I call the hospital and a Chinese doctor says so sorry him have radium planted in jaw. Come on down tomorrow and we test you with Geiger counter."

"That's awful, Jack."

It was hard to think of anything to say. No wonder he was worried. He took another swallow of his drink. Then he clutched frantically at his groin and shrieked in a falsetto voice:

"Oh, doctor! Tell me it's not too late!"

"Take it easy," I told him.

I didn't think he'd clown like this if it were really serious; Werner always liked to exaggerate. But he kept on this way for a while, imitating the sound the Geiger would make when they put it to him, shouting that he was a walking uranium mine, and so on. At last he caught me glancing at my watch.

"What's your problem?" he asked.

"I came here to get some information. I want to find out about mausoleums."

"For instance?"

"Do they have locks on the doors?"

He looked at me in a funny way. "Yes. Probably Yale locks, most of them."

"How are the bodies kept inside?"

"All kinds of ways. Some are in tombs on the floor, some are in crypts in the wall. Sometimes they have a sarcophagus—"

"Is that one of those big things?"

"Yeah. It's just a stone vault that's above the ground, for people who don't like ground burial. Why are you asking about this?"

"I'm writing a book on funeral customs."

"No crap, what are you up to?"

"If you must know—and this is confidential—I'm on a case. You remember reading about that exhumation where the body was missing?"

"Yeah. That was a weirdie."

"I have an idea that the body was hidden in a mausoleum. I can't tell you any more. Now, what tools do I need to break in?"

His tiny eyes bugged out. "Do you *know* it was hidden in this particular mausoleum?"

"No."

"Then you're crazy!"

"Just a second, Jack. Listen to me. Suppose you were going to hide a coffin in a mausoleum. Suppose you were too cautious to hide it in your own mausoleum—even if you had one. All right. Now, would you hide it in the mausoleum of a stranger or in the mausoleum of someone you knew?"

He thought the question over, then said:

"Someone I knew."

"Why?"

"Because I could keep track of him. I'd know if he was going to have a funeral in his family. If and when he was, I'd be able to run back to the mausoleum and get the coffin before he found it."

"Exactly. It's pure logic."

"You're crazy, fella!"

After some further argument, Werner gave me the

scoop. The door to the mausoleum could be opened with a skeleton key. The marble facings over the crypts were thin and could be smashed with an ordinary hammer. For the tombs in the floor I'd need a crowbar. "But if you're talking about a sarcophagus, that's a hearse of a different color. If it's a metal cover you can get it off with an automobile jack. But if it's stone, it might weigh twelve hundred pounds. You'd have a hell of a time moving that."

"Anything else I'd need?"

"Only one thing. A straitjacket."

I sighed and said it was just one of those things. I'd gotten into a mess, one thing had led to another, and here it was the last inning, and I had to come up to bat.

"Don't do it," Werner said.

"It's no use. I have to. Is there any equipment around here I could borrow?"

"When are you going?"

"Tonight. Because if my theory is correct, then the guy who took the coffin will be coming back for it. There's another funeral coming up at this mausoleum in a day or two."

"Then it's too late, Clem. Look at the time. Let's face it: if somebody's going there tonight, he's beaten you already. Besides, do you know where this particular mausoleum is located?"

"No."

"Then how could you find it? You want to be stumbling around in the dark looking for it, and with no equipment, nothing?"

What he said made sense. I asked how he'd go about it.

"I'd go there early tomorrow and take a look—see if anything's been disturbed recently. Maybe the coffin never was there in the first place. Maybe it was there, but by now it's been taken away.

"Okay. If you think it's still there, you bring back the equipment in a car and hide it nearby. Better yet, hide the car there. Then at night, when everyone's gone, you move in."

"I guess you're right," I said.

"But I still wouldn't do it."

His face was earnest now and, for a minute, the yarmulka didn't look so out of place. As he took another quick swallow of his drink, the ice cubes bobbed about in the glass, nudging each other familiarly. The phone rang. He picked it up. "Yes, Rabbi . . . that's for eleven o'clock tomorrow . . . yes . . . goodnight, Rabbi."

I thanked Werner, pledged him to silence and got up to leave. When I was at the door he called me back. He asked if I knew that coffins had locks.

"No."

"Well, they do. The Christian ones, I mean. We have mostly rowboats and flattops here, but the metal coffins have bolts that slide back inside. We call them sealers. Just a second."

He rummaged around in the drawers of his desk. "I'm sure I saw one—here it is." In his freckled hand was a metal tool about six inches long. It looked like a miniature version of the cranks they used to start the old-time cars.

"You'll find a small hole in front of the coffin, just under the lid. You stick this thing in and turn it, and the bolt will slide back."

"Thanks, Jack."

"Not at all. I wouldn't want you to break into a vault and not be able to open the coffin."

"You always were thoughtful."

"Not at all and, Clem, remember one thing."

"Yes?"

"You're taking on a grave responsibility."

20

The rain had started again.

It was the same rain that had begun in the early afternoon, letting up later when Helen and I went to see Andresen. Now it was back, a cold drizzling winter rain that made the streets black and shiny.

A feeling of nostalgia as I trudged away from the Montefiore Zionist Chapel. On other nights, in younger days, I'd left this same funeral home and walked these same streets under the glow of what had passed for happiness at the time. When Werner and I were young and broke and out on a double date, sometimes we'd end the evening with a session here where there were always soft couches and soft lighting, eternal quiet and plenty of ice cubes.

How cheap can you get?

Well, it had been a long time ago and we never had any dough in those days. The girls hadn't minded—the first time. Where else could we go? We didn't have the money that all the kids have nowadays.

Some of them were passing in their new cars now, slithering over the black shiny pavement. In most of the cars there was just the lone driver, and it's always this way in the city in the early-morning hours.

It makes you wonder.

If you walk through the streets and watch, you see hundreds of cars riding about aimlessly and the young white faces stare out at you through the glass. And on nights like tonight, with the rain running down the windows and the light splintered and refracted by the moving drops of water, these young white faces look even wilder and more distorted and more lost than usual.

Sometimes I thought of them as a lost army, an army of the lost, rejects, dropouts, drifters. Here they were—with no jobs, no girls, no nothing—just roaming around in the rain. It made me uncomfortable and I'll tell you why:

When I was in college I learned that there's only one basic plot—the search, the quest—and that every book involves a search for something, whether it's a woman or justice or success or identity or the Holy Grail. And even though people make fun of the picture where Humphrey Bogart keeps saying, "Play it again, Sam," and the guy sings:

> *"It's still the same old story,*
> *A fight for love and glory—*

there was a lot of truth in it. Even my own activities, far out as they were, were in the main current. Maybe it was odd to be looking for coffins and dead bodies, but at least I was searching for something.

To roam about aimlessly at night was much worse. Then you were in a different league, in with the Ancient Mariner and the Flying Dutchman—a man without a country, a rebel without a cause. Then you were sick, buddy, and don't say it takes one to know one.

The subway entrance was now ahead.

Four wet slippery city blocks had brought me here. The dank polluted odor hit me even before I reached it—a blind man would have known. I went underground just as a train was screeching into the station.

The subway isn't as bad as people say. It's rough during the rush hours, yes, but at night it can be a real tranquilizer. You just sit there quietly, not moving a muscle, and you get wafted along effortlessly and you watch the strange-looking characters who get on and off and you wonder about their secrets and their hidden lives. The guy sitting opposite you could be anything from an eccentric millionaire to a homicidal maniac to a member of the FBI. In every single subway car, the psychiatrists say, there's at least one person who's ready to scream.

The train hurtled into the station. Some motormen like to come in that way, jamming on their brakes at the last moment, causing sparks to fly as the metal wheels grind into the tracks.

The door closed. Again we rattled through the dark tunnel. About five or six more stops and we'd be at Concourse Square. But I'd been thinking. Maybe I ought to be more careful. After all, three men were already dead and a guy had followed me last night, a guy who could have gunned me down if he'd been the real thing. Maybe I ought to vary my routine a little to keep them guessing.

Anyway, when the train finally pulled into Concourse Square, I got off with some of the other passengers, then ducked back into the next car just as the sliding doors were closing. It was real private badge stuff.

I was the only one to get out at the next stop and my route home was now south rather than north. Rain was still falling. Briskly I walked the extra blocks through the factory district and then, from across the street, I paused to study the front of our building.

There was nobody in sight. A dim light lit up the vestibule. Through the glass of the outer door I could see it was empty. So were the cars parked in front of the building. As I crossed the street I noted idly that one of them, a Chevrolet station wagon, had no license plate.

Now I was in the vestibule, fumbling for my key. I peered through the inner glass door into the lobby. It, too, was deserted.

But my key didn't fit. It wouldn't go in the lock. I held it up to the light.

It was the right key.

Something made me look over my shoulder. A big man was getting out of the station wagon, a mask or something over his face—

That's when I put my arm in front of my eyes and kicked at the inner door. *Crash*! Particles of glass beat against my arm and head, a fragment sliced at my leg. Then I was backing through the gap as his arm came up. A gun. The shots caused more glass to spray into my face.

I stumbled toward the stairs—it was the only place to go. My shoes pounded up two flights. On the third-floor landing I stopped and listened.

There were soft footsteps in the lobby, none upon the stairs. Then the sounds ceased. Silence.

Where was he?

Holding my breath, I listened. Not a sound below. Some blood ran into my eye and I wiped it off. Could he be creeping up the stairs? I looked over the banister, ready to draw back if necessary, but he wasn't there. For about five minutes I waited as the silence seemed to be building up to a climax. Then a door opened somewhere below.

But I still didn't want to go down those stairs, so I climbed the remaining flights and let myself out on the roof. It was still drizzling. Puddles squished on the gravelly material beneath my feet. About twenty yards away some wild shapes waved from a clothesline, long underwear and stuff. Walking to the front of the building, I looked down and saw that the station wagon was gone. But that didn't mean he was.

Well, what now?

Only five or six feet separated me from the roof of the adjoining apartment building. I could have jumped it easily, slippery though the roof was, but I guess I was chicken. Besides, there was another way.

The fire escape.

Its metal bars and slats were glistening with raindrops. It

was a tangled mass of steel latticework, crossing and recrossing to a narrow point below. I hadn't been on one in some time.

But don't get the idea that a fire escape is safer than jumping from building to building, because it all depends on how you go about it. If you stalk down and some ex-cop or hunting enthusiast just happens to be awake, you can really get blasted. No, sir, if you're going down a fire escape at night, it's best to go hell-for-leather.

Texas-style.

Once more I looked downward. The raindrops clung to the metal scaffolding, sparkling like fireworks in the light from the streetlamp on the corner. My hands gripped cold metal—the railings of the first ladder. The way was clear. I took a deep breath. One. Two.

Now!

Pounding down the ladder to the fifth-floor platform, I made the turn. But I'd skidded on the last step and my hand had knocked against some milk bottles on a windowsill. Like pins in a bowling alley they spun and teetered, almost as if they weren't going to topple, but I've been in enough bowling alleys to know when I have a strike.

They started falling then, in easy stages, slowly at first, one by one, bouncing off the lower platforms and making more noise than the two skeletons banging on a tin roof in a hailstorm. Yet it didn't matter because it was full speed ahead, every man for himself. I was halfway to the fourth floor before the first glass fragments tinkled on the pavement below. Making a quick turn on the landing, I started down the next ladder.

Someone yelled just then, so I jumped the rest of the way, landing on some pottery and plants, and another shower of debris rained earthward. A light went on as I swarmed down toward the third floor.

Suddenly my neck was caught in some clothesline and I was choking—strangling—fighting to get free. I tore at the rope with both hands. A pulley snapped off the side of the building and the clothesline slackened. But I was still caught—now it was around my legs—I jerked at it—a scream and a cat's meow.

Somehow I made it to the last platform. Here I dropped the remaining twelve feet to the sidewalk, landing on all fours, my fingers brushing against fragments of glass. But I was okay—I hadn't broken anything—

A woman's scream was ringing through the rain as I made a wide end run around the corner of the building. Cermak the super was picking shattered tongues of glass from the shattered inner door.

"You—" he said.

"Someone tried to mug me."

"You come home all the time so late—what you expect?"

I looked at the lock. Jammed into the keyhole was something white. Splintery. A wooden match, Cermak said. "They stick it in and break it off."

"So I see."

Well, that was it. Nothing fancy. Simple but effective. Just a kitchen match and a little piece of lead. They didn't use a death ray when they went after big Clem Talbot.

21

A police car came along at this minute. It was about time. I ran out and signaled. It pulled over to the curb.

"What's up, Jack?"

"Some guys tried to mug me."

"We got a call there was someone on a fire escape."

"That was me. I ran up on the roof. Could you give me a lift to the hospital?"

"Sure. Climb in."

I sat in the back, a wire screen between me and the driver, and they took my name and pretended to believe my story. One of them called to Cermak that they'd be back. Then they drove me to the rear entrance of Concourse General Hospital, where I got out. Police cars, their red lights circling crazily, were grouped around a new ambulance, big enough for several patients and their lawyers.

More cops were staring at my bloody face.

It didn't bother me. Cops in blue you don't have to worry about. It's the ones who don't wear uniforms who are dangerous.

"Thanks for the lift," I said.

"Don't mention it, champ."

I had to wait outside the emergency room because it was Saturday night. It seemed to be trouble night for a lot of people. Sitting there on a hard wooden bench, I looked over those who were ahead of me.

It was what you might expect. A kid with a nosebleed. An old man wheezing with asthma or something. Two drunks babbling to themselves. An Esso mechanic with a bloody handkerchief around one hand. A young woman with a baby wrapped in a pink blanket.

The entrance to the treatment room was screened off by a sheet that had once been white. After about five minutes a young foreign doctor came out, glanced at my eye, and said I'd have to wait.

The woman with the baby went in. The baby started howling.

In one corner of the room a gray-haired old woman sat in an old-fashioned wooden wheelchair that looked like the phantom rickshaw. There was a big lump in the center of her forehead. "Screw you," she snarled all of a sudden.

Then a few minutes later a young black man strolled out of the treatment room with his girl. A huge turban of bandage was coiled around his head, and the red stuff soaking through it didn't seem to bother him. Arm in arm they strolled out. Feeling kind of wistful, I watched through a window as they climbed into a golden Cadillac.

"Screw you," the old woman snarled.

She didn't mean anyone in particular. The lump in the middle of her forehead was getting bigger. The corners of her toothless mouth were bent down in a mean, nasty expression.

It was my turn finally.

In the treatment room a nurse had me lie down on a table. She washed my face and put some drops in my eye. Then the doctor looked at it with a special light and said I was lucky. He put in two stitches near the eyelid. They charged me ten bucks.

Mother was watching the Late Late Show when I got home. On the screen William Powell tickled Myrna Loy's bare shoulder with his mustache. I tried to keep my face in the shadows, but it was no use. Mother asked about my eye.

"Nothing. A slight accident."

"You won't be satisfied until you get yourself killed. Is this what all the noise was about before?"

"Yes."

"You were all right for a while and now it's started again. What kind of trouble are you in?"

"No trouble."

"Why don't you tell me? I've lived a long time."

"That doesn't mean you can solve all the problems of the world."

"Well, I know one thing—you'll never be out of a job."

"Is that so?"

"Yes. You make work for yourself."

22

That same morning, Sunday, I took a bus to St. Charles' Cemetery. My pockets were filled with hardware: dozens of skeleton keys plus a funny little gadget known as a thirty-two-caliber Smith and Wesson revolver.

The cemetery was big, taking up perhaps ten square city blocks. It was surrounded by a high iron fence spiked at the top. Two gates, the main one on the west side, where a small stone office building was located, and a service entrance at the north. Here they had a collection of shacks and greenhouses for the maintenance crew. Signs said that the gates were locked at 5 P.M.

There were no funerals, naturally, but a lot of people were around, arranging flowers on graves, sometimes kneeling to pray.

I used to think death made all men equal, that every man—rich or poor—got six feet of earth and no more. But it isn't true. Even in death, some are still on top.

You see, in a Catholic cemetery they figure that no one in a family will be cremated. Therefore, the grave has to be extra deep. It goes down ten feet and three caskets can be stacked in it. As the years go on, the caskets begin to disintegrate and the top caskets tend to sink lower and crush the guy at the bottom.

It's symbolic, sort of.

Anyway, no one bothered me. I wandered through the

rows of tombstones and markers, noting that most of the mausoleums were grouped like military pillboxes on the northern outskirts of the place. The Gilbert mausoleum I found just below a small wooded area on a hill.

It was big as these things go, a rectangular building with a front that resembled a Greek temple. It took me a few minutes to open the heavy door.

Then I was inside—in a large stone chamber—and I shut the door and used my flashlight. There was a big stone sarcophagus in the middle of the floor, big enough to hold at least two coffins. On the wall in back of it were what seemed to be large shelves in the stone, each of them sealed over with a marble plate on which names and dates were inscribed. These were the crypts.

On some of the other walls religious paintings had been done right on the stone. The paintings were crude and childlike, the round faces stacked one on top of the other like cannonballs, but they fitted in well with the medieval atmosphere. They were so bad they were good, if you know what I mean.

I flashed my light around the cold stone floor to check if the dust had been disturbed recently.

Dust?

There wasn't any.

Next I examined the sarcophagus. It was massive, formed of yellowish stone, but I thought I could handle its metal top with the proper equipment. The name Angelina Ghiberti was inscribed on the metal.

That left the four crypts. Here no recent plastering had been done; the plaster along the edges of the marble facings was powdery and discolored, aged by time, something that's hard to fake, and there were no plaster drippings on the floor.

Well, that was all I could do for now. If a coffin had been concealed here lately, it would have to be in the sarcophagus, but the absence of dust anywhere made it impossible to tell.

When I got back to the main part of the cemetery, I asked a maintenance man how often they cleaned the mausoleums.

"We keep them clean all the time."

"I mean the insides."

"That's up to the families. Some families pay special to have them cleaned every month. Most folks don't bother."

"I see." Someone had bothered.

I left then, remembering that gravediggers were said to have the best job in the world. They started at the top and worked down.

The next stop was a private garage. It was no use going to Hertz Rent-a-Car or their rivals because my name would be on a blacklist. After all, my last rental had been burned up with a couple of bodies in it.

The guy asked thirty dollars to rent a Jeep station wagon.

"I don't want to buy it—I just want to use it for a day."

"This is a special car, Mac. It's got four-wheel drive, automatic transmission, power steering—"

"Any car I'm driving has power steering."

"Not like this car."

"I'll give you twenty dollars and bring it back with a full gas tank."

"Full of what?"

I laughed.

"Make it twenty-five," he said, "and leave the gas tank alone."

About four that afternoon, dressed in work clothes, I drove through the main gate. The back of the Jeep was loaded with mechanical gear, the latest equipment. This job would take more than Boris Karloff and a couple of shovels.

No one challenged me. They never do if you look like you're working.

Down the service road I went, slowly, my eyes checking the burial grounds on both sides. I cruised near the wooded heights by the Gilbert mausoleum. There were people there, so I had to keep going. Turning to the left, I parked on a side road and waited about twenty minutes until a warning bell sounded—the signal that the gates would soon be locked.

I turned the Jeep around. Now I was again cruising near the mausoleum, slowing up for a last panoramic inspection of the terrain.

Nothing moved, except some small trees and bushes harried by the wind. No visitors. No maintenance crew. Even the birds had left. It was just me and the dead.

With the Jeep in four-wheel drive, I charged up the hill like Teddy Roosevelt at San Juan; I could almost hear the bugles. The whine of the four-wheel drive was interrupted by the whipping of small branches across the windshield. Crashing through some small shrubs, braking sharply to avoid a rock, I twisted into a small space among some trees.

A regular car wouldn't have made it.

It may sound paradoxical, but this is the kind of car you need in the city, especially if you're a woman. Women would never hear of it, of course, because they go in for those cute little sport cars. But what good is a car like that against the creeps who prey on women driving alone?

They'll sideswipe a woman's car on some lonely street as a pretext to get her to stop. Or they'll jump in front of her at a stop sign and refuse to budge. Sometimes they pretend to have lost something under her car—they lie down and make out they're looking for it—and then say she has to pay them for the loss.

A car like the Jeep, a car with high ground clearance, this is the answer. All you do is drive right over them and keep on rolling along.

There was nothing to do but wait. I sat there for a few hours, smoking an occasional cigarette as it became darker and the cold crept through the woods. At six-thirty the traffic rumble beyond the trees had lessened. The beast was feeding. Soon it would be time for me to make my move.

About half an hour later I turned the key in the ignition and the motor came to life. Around me the trees stood dark and implacable, and they couldn't care less. A big white moon was floating in the dark vault of the sky; some clouds smeared themselves over it and the trees were darker still.

Slowly I backed the wagon out of the woods, turned it around and eased it down the slope toward the mausoleum that stood there, blocklike in the gloom. The Jeep jounced back on the service road, stopped near the wooden door.

My key turned grudgingly in the lock. The door opened on blackness. Now the yellow beam from my electric lantern bounced about the stone chamber, sketching in the sarcophagus, the tier of crypts, and the paintings on the wall.

I went inside.

It was very cold. My footsteps were noisy on the stone floor. I set down the lantern so that its light focused on the horizontal crevice at the side of the sarcophagus, the line marking the position of the cover.

The cover fitted better than I'd realized. But the chisel in my hand was sharp as well as cold. I stuck it in the crevice and pushed downward, and the crack widened. But now what? I'd forgotten to bring wedges.

I had to improvise. My left hand fumbled in a pocket and closed over some coins. The dimes and pennies fitted in the crack. I stuck the chisel in at another point below the cover and repeated the procedure—a kid playing with a row of slot machines. But the crack was wider now, a black line etched on the side of the tomb.

Little by little I added other coins, putting them in stacks of twos and threes, inching up the cover. When the space was wide enough for the automobile jack, I began cranking. The metal cover moved upward.

A noise behind me.

In the crypts, it sounded like. But when I swung around there was nothing there. Each marble facing was smooth and cold, each occupant's name clearly inscribed on each pink-veined surface. It was ridiculous to look for anything in this direction. And yet, I'd heard something—I couldn't be mistaken.

Perhaps an echo from outside?

I switched off the lantern, its last rays catching the crude paintings on the walls, those round faces with the painted eyes, and, removing my shoes, I tiptoed to the door, unmindful of the cold stone beneath my feet because I was groping in my pocket for the thirty-two. Opening the door cautiously, I peered into the night.

I could see nothing there but the Jeep. The moon was throwing a few candlepower on some nearby tombstones. Nothing moved except a few clouds, high up in the night sky. I waited, my body pressed against a column, my feet freezing on the stone, straining my ears for some sound other than the steady marching of my heart.

Nothing. Nobody. A gust of wind, a rustle of some naked shrubbery. Yet there had been a noise. I tried to recall what it had been like.

It was a relief to get my shoes on again. The lantern flared and the painted faces stared into mine, blank and solemn, their big eyes dark against a soft yellow background. They didn't bother me. The jack was still in position, so I cranked some more.

The cover moved upward. It cleared the top of the sarcophagus. Inside I saw a metal coffin. It was up high—as if on top of something—and there was only one person listed for this tomb.

This had to be it.

Grabbing the cover with both hands, I lifted carefully, just to test its weight. It was heavy but I could handle it. I slid it off slowly, leaning it against the sarcophagus, and then I used my flashlight again. Sure enough, there were two coffins in there, the bottom one collapsed and rotten.

Some grubby bones and rags were visible—the remains of Angelina Ghiberti.

The top coffin was made of a dull gray metal, neither shiny nor rusted, and it was impossible to tell how long it had been there. Bending over the sarcophagus, I reached down with my left hand, feeling for an opening just below the coffin lid. There it was—as Werner had said it would be—a small round hole.

Now I fumbled through my pockets for the coffin opener, that odd little crank that looked like something from a Model T. It fitted easily into the hole, engaging the locking mechanism, and, as I turned it, I felt something give.

Carefully I raised the lid.

But it was like a Chinese puzzle. Inside the coffin was a long wrinkled metal bag that could have been fashioned from zinc. I cut through the thin sheet metal with difficulty, careful not to hurt myself. Pungent, stinging fumes vaporized up into my throat and nostrils, choking me for a second, and I had to stop. Preservative solution, harsh and powerful, not the Chianti wine which Gilbert had claimed they used in Europe.

The fumes spread. It was like being tear-gassed. I had to fall back a few steps, but I couldn't wait. Holding my breath now, I was back tearing at the metal flaps with both hands.

A man's body—naked because there had been no funeral. The body of Sebastian J. Lo Curto. A row of black stitches down the abdomen. The skin was a hard leather, but beneath it I could feel something rounded and firm.

When I cut the stitches the abdomen gaped open as if anxious to give up its secret. Reaching into the clammy belly, my fingers closed over a large plastic cylinder. I pulled it out. It was a canister almost a foot long, maybe four inches in diameter, grayish in color and dripping with the preservative. After wiping it dry, I unscrewed the plastic top.

A fine white powder. I dumped some on my shoulder and licked at it like a cat. It was bitter, like heroin or quinine. Replacing the top, I put the canister down. In front of me the abdomen was a gaping hole. There was no way to sew it up. Instead I tried to drag the cut edges of the metal bag together. The thin metal puckered and squeaked.

Just then I noticed something else.

My tongue. It felt wooden. I ran it along my teeth. Something was wrong with it. It was becoming numb like at the dentist's. Local anesthesia. This white powder was cocaïne

No wonder the mob had been concerned. This was for the high-class addicts, those who could afford fifty dollars a shot. Bankers, executives, show-business characters, the big wheels. It made their big brains work better. And it was much more expensive than heroin.

There had to be at least several pounds in this canister. At eight hundred grand a pound, that would be several million dollars.

It didn't take me too long to tidy up. First I closed the coffin over the metal bag, not bothering to lock it. Then I reached for the cover of the sarcophagus, the end that was resting on the floor, tilted it, and began schlepping it back. Man, it was heavy.

Boom!

A gun or something went off behind me—

But I wasn't hit—I hadn't felt anything—and when I swung around there was no one in the gloom.

I picked up the lantern and flashed its beam around wildly. The walls, the painted faces, they all looked the same. But there was a terrible odor in the room now, much worse than the embalming fluid, and as the light moved up the wall I saw something on the crypt at the top—a big star-shaped hole in the marble facing that hadn't been there before.

A faint sighing noise from above.

Then some brown liquid appeared at the jagged rim of this hole and began to dribble silently down the wall.

23

I got out of there fast.

The heavy door slammed shut behind me and I found myself in the Jeep, driving up the hill. All my gear was left in the mausoleum. I hadn't replaced the cover of the sarcophagus; the shattered crypt and the stolen coffin must still be facing each other in the feeble light.

Not that I'd panicked exactly. I knew there was nothing in that crypt that could ever hurt me. It must have been the nervous strain of the past week, the mounting tension and worry, the murder of Gilbert. All this and then that odor, that sudden overpowering smell of death, and some animal thing inside me had cried *go!*

Miraculously, I'd brought the canister along. My fingers felt for it on the seat beside me, gripped it tightly as the trees outside the Jeep whispered of millions of dollars.

I looked around. There was nobody here. Nobody knew I had the canister. Up above the moon dimmed momentarily, a 30-watt bulb in a smoky backroom, and a voice was whispering:

This is it, Talbot, this is really it. It's still the script only it's the happy ending this time. You don't have to travel second class any more. You don't have to do other people's dirty work. It's all up to you.

Think it over, Talbot. It's reel 5, only someone made a mistake and put in the happy ending. This is your big chance and it will never come again. You've got a fortune there and you've got a gun. You can walk out of here right now and blast anyone who gets in the way.

I couldn't argue with the voice: it had all the good arguments. My only recourse was some thought-saving action. And so, getting out of the wagon, I opened the canister. Then I walked around the woods, scattering the powder about and watching the white grains flash in the moonlight before they disappeared forever. So much for that.

Some may think me a chump, others a hero. But keep the Boy Scout medal. I acted out of self-interest. Yes, I could have walked out of there with the cocaine, but I'd only be walking into more trouble. I'd still be holding the bag—even if it was a bag of gold.

Besides, everything else was secondary at this point. The main job wasn't over. I'd really come to the cemetery to find the killer.

Last night he'd tried to kill me—he might try again. It was up to me to stop him if I could. And if I walked out of here now—with or without the shipment—I'd be losing the best chance I'd ever have to do just that.

Because he didn't know it was too late. He didn't know the shipment was gone. He only knew that tomorrow was Gilbert's funeral—and the sarcophagus might be opened. That's why he'd have to come tonight.

And when he came, I'd be waiting for him. A show-down. A final reckoning. We'd settle it here tonight in the loneliest spot in town, and I was betting on me.

To get a better view, I turned the Jeep around. The mausoleum was about a hundred yards down the slope. I could see it clearly, a dark mass with those heavy columns in front now bleached white by the moon. They made a perfect backdrop before which he'd have to pass. I'd see him easily if the moon stayed out.

I felt in my pocket for the thirty-two. It was ready. Six bullets. Six lead slugs, a cross filed into each one. Six dumdums.

A bottle of beer and a sandwich helped pass a little time. I turned on the car radio, then snapped it off. Who knows? The sound might carry because of some acoustic freak here on this windy hill.

My glance shifted. My eyes, up to now fixed on the mausoleum, ranged out over the cemetery, trying to follow the outline of the service road. But it was far off, a gray and indistinct thread, lost among the trees and tombstones, with no sign of life on it.

Was he really going to come?

The sky darkened. It was only temporary, for the clouds that had upstaged the moon were moving too fast. Soon they moved off, erased like chalk smudges from a blackboard, and the burial grounds emerged from the shadows. Below me the rows of tombstones stretched into the night, milestones to nowhere, and cold gusts of wind beat downward from the hill. A good place for a murder. The best.

In my pocket the thirty-two was a hunk of ice.

The gun law is a funny thing. I didn't have a permit for the thirty-two and, therefore, I was breaking the law. But if you do have a permit for a gun, it's against the law to carry it unloaded.

Figure that out.

I had the gun because, despite my size, I've never claimed to be a tough guy. Actually, there's no such animal. A tough guy is just a man with an edge. It may be size or strength or combat skill. It may be money or influential friends or a squad of goons. It can even be education or a professional degree, something that people like Hendriques or James Lo Curto would use to put the screws on simpler folks. But it's always an edge, something extra, and a thirty-two is one of the best.

Once more the clouds straggled silently across the moon. The tombstones began to fade. I waited.

Then I saw something. A light at the far end of the cemetery. Some trees were in the way, but the light seemed to be moving, coming my way, blinking now and then as trees or tombstones intervened. Someone was coming up the service road.

The light was moving slowly. It blinked and flickered. As it moved along it lit up only small segments and patches of the ground below. It was moving toward the place where the right-hand turn led to the mausoleum.

A whitish light, dim and feeble. A flashlight, probably. It didn't swing back and forth like a lantern. Whatever it was, it kept coming.

I watched it draw nearer to the turn. It had to be the killer. Who else would come here on a Sunday night? On any night? He must have come in over the wall.

Nearer still.

The beam was brighter now and directed downward. A flashlight. It was tracing the gray outline of the road like a slow but steady hand, moving from left to right, never pausing. It was coming to the turn. I'd see him as he came around the corner.

I found myself holding my breath. The light was almost at the turn. In a moment he'd come into view. But just then, the light went out. Darkness over the road.

Had he made the turn?

I didn't know. I couldn't see anything now. But he must have turned the corner. The moonlight wasn't strong enough to outline the path through the tombstones, but he'd be visible when he reached the mausoleum. Somewhere below he padded silently over the graves, his feet noiseless on the dead grass, a figure lost in shadow. He was creeping quickly from one tomb to the next, well hidden by the stones and statuary, pausing now and then to listen, crouching behind a tombstone as he listened, cautious and wary, but all the time working his way toward that big wooden door.

The moon began to fade.

My eyes were searching the darkness below and I was beginning to see things that couldn't be real moving about in the shadows. I blinked my eyes but it didn't help. Foggy shapes formed and vanished and re-formed at the fringes of the mausoleum. If only the moon would come back to whiten the walls and columns there. If only the clouds would give the moon a chance. But then I saw a glint of something like metal, and a vertical shaft of yellow light momentarily outlined the edge of the wooden door.

He was inside.

I got out of the wagon and started down the slope, the thirty-two in my hand. The mausoleum wasn't so far away—a sprinter could have made it in seconds. But I wanted to give him a minute to find out that the shipment was gone. If I timed it right, I'd get him on the way out.

Halfway down the hill I speeded up. He'd be coming out any second now.

And so he was. The door of the mausoleum swung open in a blaze of lurid light. The lanterns within exposed the nightmarish figure now emerging, a sight so fantastic and unexpected that I stopped short then and there.

It was Death's Dark Angel—a figure all in black with the shoulders hunched upward as if the night wings had been folded. I was close enough to see his imposing height, his chalk-white face, his dark glasses, and the naked body in his arms.

And for a second I thought I knew him as some little trick of posture or movement, some gesture, almost gave him away. But then it was gone and he was Death's Dark Angel again, and he was taking the body away.

24

I started to run, carefully at first until the momentum got me, and then I was going faster and faster, gripped by the exhilaration of speed and downhill rush, and I didn't care any more. I wanted to fly, to cover the ground in great leaps and strides, and nothing mattered now except to leap on him and tear off his disguise—

Then I was falling. I'd tripped over something big and heavy. My foot.

I hit the ground hard, the breath was knocked out of me, and lights flashed behind my eyes. I hit my head also, and my knees were scraped and raw. My hand no longer held the thirty-two. Even so, as I lay there gasping for air, I still managed to look down the slope.

Yellowish lantern light still streamed from the mausoleum but the tall figure was gone. A chill wind swept through the dry grass in which I lay. The ground was very cold and I felt alone. Yet, more than anything else, I had a feeling of wonder, of disbelief.

Had he actually taken the body?

It was five minutes more before I could sit up. Then I was on my feet, searching for the thirty-two, and I couldn't find it. But suddenly a thought came to me—I didn't need the gun any more. He could easily have killed me just now, when I was down and helpless, if that's what he had wanted.

But he hadn't tried to kill me tonight. He hadn't even come up the hill to look for the shipment. It didn't make sense. It didn't add up with what had gone before: the plot to steal the shipment, the murder of Gilbert, the attempt on my life. All he'd seemed to be interested in was the body that he'd carried away. Maybe he really was Death's Dark Angel—

Impossible.

Just the same, I went down to the mausoleum to check. Sure enough, the body of Sebastian J. Lo Curto was gone. It hadn't been a dream. Whoever or whatever had come here had taken it away to God knows where, and the mystery was greater than before. Too tired to think, too tired to pick up the lantern and the rest of my gear, I closed the mausoleum door, turned around and clumped up the hill.

I'd blown it.

Now I was sitting in the Jeep once more. I turned on the radio, I switched if off. Music brings regret and that I didn't need. What's more, an idea was taking form in my mind.

Actually, there'd been something in the back of my mind for a long time. It was nothing definite, just some subconscious impressions, a few vague associations that suggested a pattern of some sort—nothing you could put your finger on. However, there was something.

You know what I mean. A feeling that you have the pieces of the puzzle but you can't quite join them together.

I had that feeling now. I knew there was something, a quicksilver thing that had so far failed to take shape. Yet now, just as you go to sleep with a problem and wake up with the answer, the fall seemed to have shaken the pieces into a pattern.

Maybe I hadn't blown it. There was another angle and there was still time to check it out tonight, even at this ungodly hour. On the East Side of Manhattan was a hospital where I could go.

A special kind of hospital, the only one of its kind that's

open for emergencies twenty-four hours a day. It operated like that because the rich live on the East Side and, when they want service, they're willing to pay.

That's where I'd go.

To a dog and cat hospital.

25

By the time I got to the funeral home it was well after midnight. The front door was dark, but light from a streetlamp spelled out the name *SCATOLOGGIA* on the big sign. James Lo Curto, whom I'd phoned from the veterinary hospital, was waiting in a car by the curb.

"Did you bring a gun?" I asked.

"Yes."

We went around to the back alley. A station wagon stood there, poorly outlined by the light coming from under the embalming room door. Lo Curto right behind me, I tiptoed over to the door, jerked it open, and stepped inside into a white glare. At the porcelain table Karl was bending over a body.

A man's body with a long autopsy incision that ran down chest and abdomen to expose the empty body cavity. It looked like the body from the mausoleum but it wasn't.

It was Gilbert.

His face had been fixed up remarkably well. The features, seemingly shattered beyond repair by the fall to the pavement, had been restored to normal. They held a peaceful expression. Even the gaping incision could not detract from the overall effect. It was a masterpiece.

"What is this?" Karl asked. His pale eyes shifted back and forth between me and Lo Curto.

"Hello, Karl," I said.

He just kept on working. From Gilbert's neck a rubber hose led to the suction pump which was whirring harshly. Pink fluid gurgled into a catch bottle. Fiddling with the tube in Gilbert's neck, Karl grumbled:

"They always cut the carotids too short."

I had to admire his cool. I said I wanted to ask him something.

"Yes?"

"What is it when a marble crypt explodes?"

"Oh, that. In the trade we call it a blowout."

"What causes it?"

"The gases accumulate. It doesn't happen in the new vaults because they have built-in air vents."

"I see."

"Is that why you came here?" he asked, raising his voice above the whirring of the pump.

"No. I came to wrap this case up."

"What case?"

"Don't play dumb. I saw you at the mausoleum tonight. I know you took the body at the airport. You had me fooled all along with that red wig."

Lo Curto broke in to ask what I meant.

"The red wig was a red herring. It was meant to distract attention from the sunglasses. The wig was such an obvious disguise it made me assume that the sunglasses were a disguise also."

"Well, weren't they?"

"No, they were a necessity. The man who stole the coffin had weak eyes that were sensitive to the sun. It was high noon when he went to the airport so he had to wear dark glasses. His eyesight was so lousy that he banged his car into the warehouse. He couldn't even sign the bill of lading on the right line."

"But that wouldn't prove this man was the thief," Lo Curto said.

"No, but it would have made me look for someone with weak, sensitive eyes. I'd have noticed that Karl wore tinted glasses. I'd have noticed how pale his eyes were and how they jumped from side to side, and how he was always the last to recognize me when I came to the funeral home. I wouldn't even have had to know he was an albino."

"An albino?"

"Yes. You see how pale he is. He's an albino and albinos have lousy eyesight. But I never figured any of this out. It came to me subconsciously—"

The lawyer said he didn't understand. At the porcelain table Karl was still working on Gilbert.

"You see," I continued, "in the back of my mind there was always a connection between whiteness and blindness. I mean, like in snow blindness and fog and maggots and the things that live at the bottom of the sea. But even when I was in jail—thanks to you, Lo Curto—with the rats coming after me, I didn't stop to ask why you never saw white rats except in captivity."

"You mean they're albinos?"

"Exactly. They have poor eyesight. They can't compete with the other rats. The vet told me this tonight at the cat and dog hospital."

"I can compete," Karl broke in.

"Up to now."

He didn't answer. He turned off the pump and removed the catch bottle, substituting another that contained clear fluid. After twisting some dials he restarted the pump. Formaldehyde vapor stung my eyes. Lo Curto coughed and moved back.

"In one way, it wasn't a bad plan," I said. "If Karl had been recognized anywhere along the line, the signals would have been off and he could have taken the coffin to the funeral home."

"Got it all figured out, haven't you?" Karl said.

"Just about."

I stood close to him, ready for possible trouble. The trocars gleamed on the nearby wall; it would be no trick at all for him to run one of them into me. But Karl made no such move. He was, after all, something of an artist and his immediate concern was Gilbert—his masterpiece.

Now he turned to a box marked COTTON WASTE. Two great handfuls of a fibrous gray wadding went into Gilbert's abdomen. The pump was whirring loudly. To more handfuls as Lo Curto, a little green around the gills, backed up toward the opposite wall.

But Gilbert's face was beginning to swell—it was being blown up like a tire. Karl didn't seem to have noticed—

"You've ruined him!"

My cry made Karl start. He darted a look at Gilbert's face and neck, now blown up out of all proportion like a Frankenstein's monster. Shutting off the pump, he admitted:

"Too much."

"You've ruined him."

"No. I can press some of that fluid out."

"They'll have to call in Clive Andresen."

"No—no, we don't need him."

Karl was disconnecting something in the neck. He tied off the carotid artery with a piece of string as Lo Curto watched in fascination. Now he stuffed more cotton waste into the abdomen before reaching for a pile of old newspapers. *Yanks Win in 10th, 3—2.*

Now he was spreading sheets of paper over the cotton wadding, firming it up, giving it shape. *Russia in New UN Move.*

Absorbed in the goings-on, I almost forgot why I was there. But I could never leave Gilbert here in his present condition. He was really loused up.

From a nearby surgical table Karl had picked up a length of heavy black thread. On one end of it was a big curved needle such as an upholsterer would use. He began sewing up the incision.

Russia in New UN—

The skin was being pulled together over the newspapers. Swiftly, rhythmically, Karl's fingers executed some kind of lockstitch.

Russia in—

The headline was disappearing. Long, powerful fingers thrust the needle through the skin, whipped the thread across, tightening up the slack. The headline disappeared.

Gilbert was a big football.

"All right, Karl," I said like the Scotland Yard men do in the movies.

"All right yourself."

A voice behind me. I turned my head to find Lo Curto covering me with a huge automatic. It looked big enough to hold about ten .357 Magnum cartridges—the ultimate weapon.

"I meet some simple people in my profession," the lawyer said, "but you are the simplest."

"What do you mean?"

"Talbot, didn't you have brains enough to see that I didn't—I repeat, did not—want my brother's body found?"

"But—"

"Why do you think Karl took it from the mausoleum tonight?"

"I don't know."

"Because I'm paying him to get rid of it permanently."

"You're insane."

"I don't think so, Talbot. It was in my interest not to get the body back. I had a million-dollar lawsuit going for me—a blue-chip case—against the funeral home and their insurance company. I couldn't lose unless some schmo like you found the body."

"Yes."

My voice sounded weak, beaten, stupid.

"When I got the first phone call offering to return the body, I thought it might be you. I came to your office and said I'd prosecute even if the body were returned. Then I put you in jail to teach you a lesson.

"But while you were in jail the same voice phoned a second time. He was surprised when I said I'd pay him to get rid of the body. We met and it was Karl, of course. We agreed on a price. But then you came and said you'd found out that DiMaio was in back of the original plan. I knew then that, sooner or later, you'd catch up with Karl."

"So?"

"It called for a change in tactics," Lo Curto went on. "I decided to make a deal with Gilbert. We'd give him back the shipment because neither Karl nor myself wanted any part of the drug racket. I went to Gilbert's apartment while he was cooking dinner for you."

"So you were there?"

"Yes, and Gilbert was willing to deal. But I made one mistake: I told him the coffin was in the sarcophagus in his own mausoleum. How did I know his mother was in it also? I never thought he'd go berserk on me. I guess he had a mother complex. He was a *Calabrese*—a thickhead. He tried to strangle me."

"You killed him?"

"Yes. I was lucky. I managed to grab something and hit him on the head. The blow killed him. He wasn't breathing when I threw him out the window. But now I'd killed someone from the mob. Now I really had to worry about you and your investigations."

The embalming room was silent. Whiteness gleamed from everything: the walls, the tile floor, the porcelain table, the sheets and the bloated body. Even Karl, pallid and motionless in his surgical gown, blended into the background. The lawyer and I faced each other like two silhouettes.

"Well," I mumbled, "now I see."

None of it would have happened except that DiMaio had tried to use me for an alibi. While Karl was hiding the body of Sebastian J. Lo Curto in Gilbert's mausoleum, DiMaio had flashed a switchblade at my office, expecting me to send him to jail or to the hospital. Instead, I'd overreacted. Exit DiMaio.

From then on it got complicated. Karl tried to sell the body to James Lo Curto, who tried to make a deal with Gilbert, who got himself killed—

"Yes, that's just it. Now you see."

The big automatic was still pointed at me. It never wavered. I blurted out:

"Look, that doesn't mean I'm going to tell. If you killed Gilbert in self-defense, why should I make trouble?"

"I'm sorry, Talbot."

"Even if people found out, you could get off easy. You said you had friends in the right places. It wasn't premeditated murder."

"Turn around."

"Wait. Karl—you're in the clear. You haven't killed anyone. Are you going to let him do this?"

The embalmer hadn't heard me. He was looking at the monstrous caricature of Gilbert that lay upon the table. The thing looked like Gilbert, for the features had been restored with uncanny skill, but the head and neck seemed ready to burst, like one of those inflated rubber animals that float above a Macy's parade. Gently, lovingly, Karl's fingers moved over the ruined masterpiece.

"Karl!" I said. "Don't let him do this. You're still in the clear."

The embalmer looked up. His pale eyes were dull. All he said was:

"I can compete."

"Turn around," Lo Curto said. "I missed you the other night. I can't miss here."

My palms were sweating. The barrel of the big gun had come up and was now pointing directly at my heart. One of those .357 Magnums at this range would blow a hole in my chest big enough for a man's arm.

I began to turn around. What else could you do?

26

The pain seemed to be part of the blackness. It was a long time before I remembered that I was Clem. The pain was in the back of my head, but that was all wrong because the pain was on top, somewhere in the darkness. More time passed before I realized that I was face down.

I was face down in a dark place and I couldn't move. A damp musty odor like dirty laundry or a mildewed awning surrounded me. It was warm and sickening. Lo Curto's face came back. Lo Curto and Gilbert and Karl.

My arms were tight against my sides and I couldn't bring up my legs. There was a heavy weight on my back. My fingers alone were free and they clutched at some narrow pipes that ran along each side of my body.

Where was I?

My eyes were opening and closing, my eyelids moving. Tears formed then and ran down my nose. There was a darkness, nothing but darkness at first, yet a little while later some light—very faint—was coming above.

The sticky thing over my mouth was adhesive tape, a real professional job. "M-m-m-m-m-m-m-m-m." The noise in my mouth couldn't get out past the tape. I tried again. "M-m-m-m-m-m-m." I listened for some answering sounds. There were none.

But the light was still there. It made me feel better. I

couldn't tell if it was artificial or real, but it didn't matter. Just that it was there.

Being face down made it doubly hard to get my bearings. I tried to move my arms, kick out with my feet, but it was useless. Again my fingers gripped the pipes alongside me. I must be tied to them.

But whatever they were, they couldn't be metal because they weren't cold. The fingertips of my right hand moved over a smooth rounded surface—my fingernails gouged into wood. These were wooden poles, something like broomsticks, only thicker.

Could they be oars?

I might be in a boat and that would explain the musty tarpaulin odor, the odor of cloth that's been exposed to weather time and time again. The fabric was definitely heavy, some kind of canvas, that was for sure.

Now I listened for the sounds of water, the cries of seagulls, the sound of a ship's bell. But there were no sounds and, what's more, no rocking, no motion.

But a boat doesn't have to rock if it's in drydock in a boathouse or a boatyard, or if it's beached somewhere. Somewhere there could be a boat, maybe in the salt marshes of Jamaica Bay or Canarsie, a boat drawn up on the dirty yellow-gray sand, half hidden by the tall yellow reeds, a boat that wouldn't rock until the tide came in. And if there was such a boat, and I was on it, then there was no doubt as to my ultimate destination.

The bottom of the sea.

It was the murmur of the voices that clued me in. Not the words or the voices themselves, because I couldn't hear anything distinctly, but the rhythm, the chant of statement and response, a prayer, a litany.

The Prayers for the Dead.

This didn't frighten me because these prayers weren't for me—I wasn't dead, not yet. These prayers had to be for someone else, probably for Gilbert. It was his funeral day. They were going to put him in that fancy mausoleum.

These prayers must be for him and that meant that I was still in the funeral home, probably hidden away in some closet or utility room where no one would come looking, safe for the time being. But once these people praying here had left, once the funeral was under way, Karl would be coming for me.

I struggled, trying to get free.

In the distance the prayers continued. Gilbert's wife and children, all in black, clutching big silver rosaries, would be there with the mob. The rosary beads would click softly in the thin trembling fingers of the women. A hush as Mr. Primavera arrived to pay his respects. The captains and the soldiers surround him. The prayers were still going on, but how much longer? Maybe ten minutes, fifteen minutes. I had to get out now.

So I struggled some more, but I was held in on all sides. What was this thing around me, this tarpaulin and these wooden poles? If I knew, maybe I could figure a way out.

It was a body bag.

One of those stinking green canvas things they use when the *schleppers* go out to bring in a decomposed body. It's like a sleeping bag except that it has holes in it to accommodate the two wooden poles that convert it into a stretcher. It makes a very fine straitjacket also, as I was finding out. I wondered how many hundreds of dead bodies had traveled in this bag.

A body bag. I was trussed up in it, hidden somewhere in the funeral home in a place that was dark but not completely so. Because there was some light coming through the blackness—there was an opening somewhere.

A keyhole, a broken windowpane, a poorly fitting door?

The monotonous drum roll of the litany had stopped. The voices, although still muffled, were closer now and the sounds were like normal conversation. I strained to hear but

I couldn't make out the words. Then a high-pitched female voice broke through clearly:

"Why did it have to be him?—he was so good, so kind—he never hurt anybody—and the children—they're only babies yet—what are they going to to?"

The words ended in a scream. Heavy masculine tones were soothing her somewhere far away.

Once more I tried to force some cry past the adhesive, but it was no dice. They'd really done a job on me. Sweat was forming over my body as I realized that I'd never escape by my own efforts. Somebody would have to come.

But who?

The cops, maybe, if Mother had notified them that I was missing. And there were others, there had to be, who'd miss me at the funeral—I'd told Gino I was coming and Mr. Primavera would be expecting me.

"Why, God?—why?—why?"

The woman's voice once more, hysterical and piercing. A man said something to her. *"No—no—no—"* the woman screamed.

Deep and soothing male voices tried to quiet her. But then the words meant nothing because there came a thudding noise directly above me, and I was struggling with all my tremendous strength, now the strength of ten men, as the terror hit me.

I was with Gilbert in the coffin.

27

It was no use.

After a few minutes of wasted effort, my body now slimy with perspiration, the pain in my head forgotten, I stopped fighting and concentrated on calling out. It was my only chance.

My neck and cheeks bulged with the effort. I almost lost consciousness for a moment. The pressure in my head was tremendous, causing bright specks of light to dance and sparkle through the blackness behind my eyes, and I actually did force some sounds through:

"M-m-m-m-m-m-m-m-m-m-m-m-m."

But my timing couldn't have been worse. The sounds I made were lost in the sobbing and confusion above me. Sobs and shrieks echoed and reverberated through the coffin, bodies jostled against it, people threw themselves over Gilbert. The metal handles rattled with each lunge and impact. "Daddy, daddy, oh, daddy," the young voices cried and it was horrible, horrible, yet no worse than what was in store for me.

"Don't go 'way, daddy."

A girl's voice above me—Gilbert's daughter. I felt something move. It was Gilbert's body, resting on my back. And if the girl could move it, maybe I could too, just enough so she'd notice, just enough to be saved. But as I tensed for a final convulsive effort, there was a man's voice, respectful but firm, and I heard it say:

"I'm sorry, but we have to go now."

More sobs, more screams. I struggled helplessly.

The sound of the cover closing. The light was gone now. A clicking noise as the sealer bolt slid into place. Other voices, far away.

Lo Curto and Karl, how could they do this? Why would they put me alive into this coffin? They weren't that sadistic. There had to be a reason.

Of course. Lo Curto was a lawyer. He'd have all the reasons, all the angles and loopholes. In case, just in case I was found dead in this coffin some day, why then Karl would take the rap because Karl had put me here. There'd be no bullet from Lo Curto's gun.

Now I was moving. An odd sensation, a lurch followed by a floating away. Somewhere in the blackness of space I tilted. A lurch and a dip and far-off voices mumbling. A thud beneath me. The distant whispers of the pallbearers ended with the slamming of a door.

Now a vibration under me and, once again, a sensation of motion, this time smooth and steady as the hearse gathered speed.

I was on my way.

Terror came again and I struggled, knowing that I shouldn't. I'd only use up the oxygen more quickly. Besides, there was still a chance because a Mafia funeral would have to follow a ritual:

First the funeral mass and eulogy. Then the casket goes back into the hearse and the double-parked, black Cadillac limousines move off smoothly. But before going to the cemetery, the cortege would have to pass the place where Gilbert had lived.

A last look. A final salute. It would be Gilbert's last ride and I'd be taking it with him. But all this would take time, time in which my rescuers might come.

There's something funny going on here.
Yes. Let's have a look in that coffin.
No. I'm sorry, but we have to go now.

We'd been moving for maybe five or ten minutes when the motion stopped. This should be the church. I listened, meanwhile working on the adhesive tape with my tongue. I might be able to peel it off my lips.

The sound of a door opening. Banging and sudden motion. The pallbearers were dragging the coffin across the floor of the hearse. A lurch. I was conscious of wavering in midair.

Of course! The coffin had wobbled as the pallbearers staggered under the extra weight. There probably wasn't one of them who hadn't noticed how heavy it was, but they were men, afraid to speak up. If women had been schlepping this thing I'd be free already.

Again I tilted. This time I seemed to be moving upward—the stairs of a church? Soon there was a jar and a stop. A bell tinkled nearby.

Minutes later a rumbling voice began. I couldn't make out the words, but once more it was a solemn voice followed by the vague murmur of a congregation. More time passed, I couldn't say how much. A bell tinkled near me. It tinkled again.

Now the rumbling voice rolled on without interruption. A sermon or eulogy. Words that were slurred and dampened droned on somewhere near the coffin, words that were meaningless but soothing. A distant torrent, a forest waterfall.

My breathing was faster and not just from panic. The oxygen might be giving out. I could hear my breathing better now that the droning voice had stopped. My whole body was wet.

I still hadn't budged the adhesive. I was making the faces of a madman, wrinkling the skin over my jaws, contorting my features into smiles and frowns and silent laughter, my eyes bulging and my nostrils flaring in desperation. And more time was passing.

"... *fiat voluntas tua, sicut in caelo, et in terra* ... "

The new priest had a clear penetrating voice. The Latin hit me where I lived, not that I understood the words. Somehow, Latin makes things sound more final.

The final sound. Like the sound when the time lock door in the bank vault closes, and you know that they can't open it again.

Mother.

"... *et dimitte nobis debita nostra sicut et nos dimittimus nostris* ... *Et ne nos inducas in tentationem, sed libera nos a malo* ... *A-men* ... "

The final sound. That hoarse little voice that whispers that you're not going to make it.

Mother.

I hadn't been able to do anything with the adhesive. It was plastered over my mouth like a flat relentless hand that wouldn't let go. Short gasping breaths were coming through my nostrils. I heard footsteps near my head, something touched the coffin, and then there was a long sighing response from the congregation.

"... *reliquescat in pace* ... *Dominus vobiscum* ... "

For a few minutes there was silence. Then some shuffling noises just before the coffin lurched upward. We were under way again and this was the last time. Down some steps. A pause. Moving again, sliding, a thump, and a door slamming with the final sound. Then the vibration of the running gear.

Mother.

It was becoming painful to breathe. I couldn't control the short jerky gasps that caused that tight feeling in my chest. The stale mildewed odor of the body bag no longer bothered me—I wanted more of it. More air. Sweat was dripping off my face, running into my eyes, stinging and smarting. Only vaguely was I conscious of the floating motion, I didn't care about that. Just to breathe was all I

wanted, all I'd ever wanted. For thirty-eight years I'd
thought the air was free.

Mother.

I had to face it now while I could still think. I'd never
see her again unless there was a miracle. An auto accident—a
big car smashes into the hearse and overturns it—the coffin
is thrown out—it opens—

There's still a chance at the cemetery, Mother, a very
good chance. They'll find the mausoleum a shambles—the
sarcophagus already open—the stolen coffin—panic and confusion—a take-charge guu—a phone call to the cops—

Where's this guy Talbot?

There's something funny going on here.

Let's have a look in this coffin.

Yes.

That's it.

They'll save me at the mausoleum.

But I was gasping now. I pushed out my tongue as far as
it would go. If I could loosen the adhesive tape enough to
catch the slack between my teeth, I'd work it into my
mouth even if the skin came with it, even if I choked on it,
just so I could get my lips free for a shout that would sound
for miles.

Mother.

The oxygen is giving out, but I've got to hang on until
we reach the mausoleum. It can't be much further. We've
traveled a long way. We must be close to the cemetery now.
And I think we're slowing down.

Yes. We've stopped.

The door of the hearse is opening. I'm sliding along the
floor. I felt a jar just then. I think they set the coffin on the
ground. Now they'll open the mausoleum. In a minute
they'll know that there's something wrong—

Where are they?

What's happening?

Wait. . . . I hear voices coming back. Here they come.
They must have opened the mausoleum. They've seen what

a mess it is—here they are and—Yes!—they're fumbling with the cover of the coffin—I'm going to be saved!

But what was that?

A sound.

A low whining sound.

The sound of machinery. Suddenly I felt myself sinking, sinking lower and lower as the voices faded. I was going down with Gilbert into a great hollow silence.

Because they hadn't opened the mausoleum. I should have realized the mausoleum was full. They hadn't found out that something was wrong.

This was a grave. A fresh grave in a Catholic cemetery. That's why it was ten feet deep. That's why I was still going down, inch by inch, slowly and creakingly as the lowering tapes unwound. Inch by inch I was sinking into a place of cool shadow, a hole in the world.

A thud as the coffin reached the bottom, settled, and lay still. A scraping sound as the lowering tapes were withdrawn.

Now there was a tapping on the top of the coffin. Again and again the noise came. Something was falling on the cover, trickling off and running down the sides. And whatever it was, it kept falling and falling and then the noise became muffled and went away. I was out of breath and very dizzy.

Were we circling? Little white lights came at me as we whirled around. It was like a merry-go-round at night, passing the same lights over and over again. Round and round you go until the lights begin to blur, but then the music cuts out and you're gliding home.

It's cold, Mother. Mother? I don't feel anything but the cold.

Mother, I'll never see you again. I'll never see you there by the TV with the drink in your hand. I'm spinning away here and I don't want to go.

It can't be real. I'm not tied up in a coffin. I'm Clem. It's all a joke, a dream. I'm not in a coffin.

Well, am I?

I don't know. I guess it doesn't matter.

It doesn't make any difference whether I'm Clem or not. I'm no one at all. Clem is just a word. It's too late, Mother. Why did we take things so seriously? It never made any difference. Whether it was real or not, and whether anyone lived or had lived or had ever lived or was still living—it really doesn't matter now.

Mother.

I'm not afraid any more.

28

A red face against a sky of the brightest blue.

A red face with blood on the lips that were calling to me. Flannery's face.

"He's alive," Flannery's face said.

"I don't believe it."

"He's breathing, I tell you. Look at him. He just opened his eyes."

Another face was looking into mine. A young and swarthy face I'd never seen before. A stranger.

"Let's get him out of there."

Arms reached down for me. Hands gripped my shoulders.

"He's tied to something. You got a knife?"

"Of course I have a knife. Every detective has a knife. Don't you?"

Click!

Light flashed off the switchblade in Flannery's hand.

Now they were pulling down the zipper on the body bag, hauling me out of the coffin. "Easy now," a voice said. We were in the cemetery in front of an open grave. Nearby stood the mausoleum. A crowd of people formed a wavering black line, men and women in funeral clothes pressing nearer or drawing back, their white faces strained in fear and wonder. Mr. Primavera's eyes were streaming tears. The body of Gilbert, larger than life, lay on the grass and, as my eyes swept around, I saw the Jeep standing nearby on the hill.

"Thanks," I blurted out when they pulled off the adhesive. "Thanks."

I would have liked to say more, but I needed air. They cut some more ropes away from me and stretched me out on the grass.

"Take it easy," Flannery said. "All the time in the world."

Feet with polished black shoes moved in my direction. Faces were gaping at me from odd angles. Some of the mourners approached gingerly, the way people do when a dangerous animal has been caught or subdued. I heard Flannery tell them to keep back. Some of the shiny shoes retreated. Flannery was apologizing to someone:

"Sorry I had to belt you, mac, but you hit me first."

"I had it comin'. You done a great thing here."

"It's my partner who gets the credit."

"How did you know he was in the coffin?"

"It's a long story, mac. You'll read about it in the papers."

Feeling better now, I struggled to sit up and finally made it. There was a concerted gasp from the crowd. Women held on to men. An old woman sank down slowly—she looked real sick. A guy was retching by a bush.

"It's wonderful," I said. "I don't know what else to say."

"Forget it." Flannery indicated the swarthy young man. "You can thank my partner here. You owe it all to him."

"Thanks. I don't know your name—"

"Leone."

"Thanks."

Flannery squatted down on the grass near me. I could see the blue sky over his beefy shoulder. He dabbed at his bleeding mouth with a grubby handkerchief. I asked what happened to him.

176

"Oh, one of the relatives had to get physical when we came to open the coffin."

"But—how did you know?"

"Take it easy. Remember I told you we have men at the funeral homes every time they bury someone in the mob? We have them there because that's one of the few times the boys can assemble without being accused of conspiracy."

"I know."

"Well, Leone was at the services today. He had his ears open and he heard someone say that they didn't get the coffin they ordered. That sounded funny so Leone asked and found out that the coffin was really king-sized.

"He's been to a lot of funerals and he noticed that the pallbearers seemed to find this coffin very heavy—it's lucky for you you're a big fat slob."

"Muscle," I said weakly.

"Anyhow, Leone phoned me from the funeral home. As it happened, I'd been thinking about you since this Gilbert got knocked off. I asked Leone if you were at the funeral and he said no. We sent a squad car to your apartment and found out you were missing—"

"Wonderful."

"I'd say it was close, Talbot. Awful close."

I tried to stand up. At first Flannery stopped me but, when I persisted, he gave me a hand. My head was dizzy and I staggered. This time the crowd gave sort of a cheer like when a football player, injured on a play, finally gets up.

Gilbert didn't get up. All dressed up like a movie actor, he rested on the grass. I staggered over to him and fell on my knees. A last look at my friend. I touched his cold hand. His shoulders had been padded so that his head wouldn't look so big.

They really should have called in Clive Andresen.

"Let's go," I said, getting to my feet and turning away.

"What hospital you want to go to?"

"You're not going anywhere like that. Just tell us who put you in the coffin."

"I'll tell you on the way. But you have to take me to a restaurant." I took two steps, stumbled, and almost fell.

"You're nuts, Talbot. You're a glutton for punishment."

"Humor me."

"Oh, all right," Flannery sighed.

With him and Leone propping me up, I moved away from the crowd and the mausoleum. A hubbub sounded behind us. I wobbled at first, it's true, but then I got stronger. The fresh air was wonderful; what did people mean saying it was smog? Near the Cadillacs we got into an unmarked police car and Leone took the wheel.

"Take me to the Rump and Romp, driver."

"Why that dump—of all places?"

"I have to see a girl."

"I give up on you, Talbot. You're out of this world," Flannery said, shaking his head.

I told them the story as Leone breezed through traffic with an intermittent snarl from the siren. And when I fingered Lo Curto as the killer, Flannery whistled.

Not that he was afraid of Lo Curto. Whatever his faults, it had taken guts for Flannery to break up a Mafia funeral. I found out later that some big names had been present, including Carmine Lombroso, Mike (Two Tits) Malecotti, Gennaro (the Jerk) Oregano, and Cristoforo Caravaggio from the New Jersey branch of the San Filippo family. What if he'd guessed wrong?

We fell silent after that as the police car rolled through the streets of the city. It had been a hectic morning for all, expecially me. I had a chance to think.

Peering through the car's dingy windows, I saw the people. They were huddled together at the traffic crossings, their little eyes wary, their mouths emitting puffs of white into the frozen air, and some of them looked curiously back at me through the glass. I knew then that I never needed the scuba gear. I'd been at the bottom of the sea all along.

The city is the bottom of the sea. Here the strange creatures live, warped and bent by the tremendous pressure, pale and blinking in the absence of the sun. The sun doesn't get through the fluid smog that floats above the rock formations of the taller buildings. But dirt and debris get through and filter down slowly to settle on the murky bottom. Trouble is always near and the strange creatures are braced to meet it. Shy and hostile, most of them are specialized in some way so they can get by.

Sometimes the small ones puff themselves to appear bigger than they are. Others develop protective camouflage, grasping tentacles, or spines that warn off the curious. And seventy percent of them hate their lives here, but they have to stay, battered by the sounds and signals and currents that never stop.

But after a while some of them can't take it any more, and then they crawl into shells left by others. That's when you find them in the big buildings that front on Concourse Square.

And here I was with them at the bottom of the sea, and I was a little bent myself, just a little. That was why I was going to see Helen. Maybe, just maybe, she and I could get by better together.

The car let me off in front of the restaurant. I went in, phoned Mother, and got a table. It was after twelve and lunch was being served. Helen brought me a drink. When I held her hand for a second, she asked what was the matter.

"It's wonderful."

"Is it?"

"Yes."

Giving me a quizzical look, she walked away. I watched her swinging stride. She was a bit rough and tough, I guess, but she was okay. I polished off the first drink, marveling that Karl hadn't embalmed me. Well, I'd save him the trouble. As I started on the second one, Helen was back to take my order.

"What do you recommend?" I asked.

"The roast lamb is good—for here."

"I'll take it. Some more drinks, too."

"What's so wonderful?"

"Everything. The blue sky. The air we breathe. And you're wonderful and we're going out tonight."

"Have you been on Geritol or something?"

"No."

Her hands were on her hips as she studied me. I imagine that she thought I was nuts. It came to me that I had on workclothes, I needed a shave, and I must smell like a body bag or worse. I also remembered the fur coat I bought from the guy in the car. While it would never fit her, I might be able to get a trade-in on it.

"Where have you been?" I heard her ask.

"At my funeral."

I wasn't even listening to our conversation at this point. My mind was elsewhere. I could see it now. The lights. The mirrors. Gay-colored dresses. The music of Marty Nussbaum's band. Werner in his green tuxedo. And Helen—in a mink coat. Good food. Lots of drinks.

Yeah . . .

Helen and I coming in at the Morgue Man's Ball.

OTHER STEIN AND DAY BOOKS YOU'LL ENJOY:

OTHER STEIN AND DAY BOOKS

MILITARY BOOKS FROM STEIN AND DAY

			U.S.	Canada
	8035-8	**ALL THE DROWNED SAILORS** Raymond B. Lech	3.95	4.50
	8015-3	**DEATH OF A DIVISION** Charles Whiting	2.95	2.95
	8109-9	**THE GLORY OF THE SOLOMONS** Edwin Hoyt	3.95	4.95
	8100-1	**A HISTORY OF BLITZKREIG** Bryan Perrett	3.95	NCR
	8039-0	**HOW WE LOST THE VIETNAM WAR** Nguyen Cao Ky	3.50	3.95
	8027-7	**MASSACRE AT MALMEDY** Charles Whiting	2.95	3.50
	8045-5	**ROMMEL'S DESERT WAR** Samuel W. Mitcham, Jr.	3.50	3.95
	8105-2	**SALERNO** Eric Morris	3.95	4.95
	8033-1	**SECRETS OF THE SS** Glenn B. Infield	3.50	3.95
	8093-5	**SUBMARINES AT WAR** Edwin P. Hoyt	3.95	4.95
	8037-4	**THE WEEK FRANCE FELL** Noel Barber	3.95	4.50
	8057-9	**THE WORLD AT WAR** Mark Arnold-Forster	3.95	NCR

EATING TO WIN

*Food Psyching
for the Athlete*

Frances Sheridan Goulart

Whether you are a weekend athlete or a professional, whatever your age or sex, *Eating to Win*, the *original* book about sports nutrition, will teach you which foods increase your strength and stamina—and which do not. What you eat can determine whether you win or lose.

Eating to Win tells you how to win through food. It is sure to be the most indispensable piece of sports equipment you'll ever own.

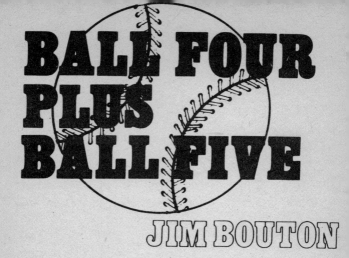

BALL FOUR PLUS BALL FIVE

JIM BOUTON

From the author who wrote the bestselling sports book of all time. Jim Bouton bares all in this updated American classic, in mass market for the first time.

"The best and funniest account I know of that strange gypsy caravan known as a ball team."

—Wilfred Sheed, *Life* magazine

"A rare view of a highly complex public profession ... ironic and courageous ... and, very likely, the funniest book of the year."

—Roger Angel, *The New Yorker*

LIZ GREENE

STAR·SIGNS FOR LOVERS

is an explicit book.

It not only shows how to interpret your own and your
partner's astrological "signature," the subtle
patterns that form a personality, but also why your
choice of lovers could be dangerous to yourself if
you ignore what is now known—and wonderfully
rewarding if you put the same information to
good and fruitful use.